A Healing Heart

By Darlia Sawyer

Written by: Darlia Sawyer
Published by: Forget Me Not Romances, a division of Winged Publications

This book is a work of fiction. Names, characters, places, and incidents are the product of the author's imagination and are used fictitiously. Any resemblance to actual events, locales, or persons, living or dead, is coincidental.

ISBN-13: 9781980577058

ACKNOWLEDGMENTS

Thank you to my publisher, Cynthia Hickey, for her understanding and patience.

Thank you to my husband, Ken. My name may be on the cover, but without his countless hours of editing, I'd be lost.

And lastly, thank you to my family and friends for your support and encouragement. My life is blessed.

Chapter One

1894

The train car door swung open as gunshots rang out. Sophie's eye's popped open as her mother screamed. Her father jumped to cover her mother with his body. He told Sophie to stay down.

A man rushed into the car his eyes wide with fear. He wore the red uniform of the train attendants. "Everyone stay seated and remain quiet! Outlaws boarded the train at the last station and have the conductor at gunpoint in the engine compartment. They're demanding the contents of the safe."

Another woman screamed and others broke down.

"Please everyone, remain calm! Don't attract attention to us. Hopefully, they'll take the money and leave. If they hear a commotion back here, they may check what's going on." Cries subsided as the attendant walked down the aisle past each bench.

Sophie's eyes locked on the car door, unaware that fear kept her from exhaling. They didn't have a way to defend themselves. The pressure building inside her caused her forced its way past her lips and she gasped for more air.

A gray-haired woman spoke up. “Sir, there are orphaned children in the rail car behind ours, did anyone warn them?”

“Yes, Ma’am. Another attendant went to tell them.”

Without warning, the train lurched forward as the brakes screeched, tossing everyone about like a ball between two boys playing catch. Sophie caught herself before she fell into her mother’s lap. Her heart pounded against her ribcage so loud she could feel it in her ears. Panic froze the faces of the surrounding passengers into strange expressions.

A distant pounding noise grew in volume outside her window and she peeked out. A gang of masked outlaws on horses neared the train. It didn’t look good. More gunshots rang out. Children from the car behind them cried. Sophie refused to speculate about what might take place if a gunman broke into their train car. Her father didn’t carry a gun. She doubted if any of the men in this car did. Sophie had wanted to learn how to handle a gun before they headed west but never followed through on it. If she had, she wouldn’t feel so vulnerable.

Her father would attract attention. He dressed every bit the influential man he was, from the tailored suit to the expensive pocket watch attached to the gold chain and his shined leather shoes. His law practice in Philadelphia was the most powerful law firm in the city. Her mother wore the latest fashions and conservative was not part of her fashion sense. Sophie wished they could change into less conspicuous clothing.

Her uncle in Texas warned them that train robberies were becoming more frequent, but Sophie never imagined it could happen to them. She assumed if robberies were increasing the presence of lawmen on trains would increase too.

Men shouting erupted outside the train. Sophie peaked out the window but couldn't understand what was being said. Two gunmen carried an injured man toward the outlaws on horses. One gunman looked toward her window and she ducked down. Curiosity could be a bad thing.

A gunman with a bandana over his face burst through the door of their car. "I need a doctor! Is anyone a doctor?"

Everyone glanced at each other, expecting someone to speak up. The silence was deafening.

The outlaw swung his gun from one side of the car to the other. "Since no one is responding, if I find out you've lied, I'll shoot you and your family."

Sophie struggled to stand but her legs gave out. Fear clenched her stomach and she could hardly breathe.

"Sit down, Sophie." Her father whispered. "You don't know what they might do to you." Charlotte, Sophie's mother, clutched her daughter's hand.

The outlaw walked toward her. "Sit down. I'm looking for a doctor, not a girl."

"I am a doctor." Sophie's voice trembled. *What am I doing? Please help me, God.*

"You're claiming to be a doctor, Now, that's funny lady." The outlaw paused, then pointed his gun at Sophie's father. "Are you trying to protect him? I don't have time for games."

"Do you think I'd draw attention to us if it wasn't true? I'm not playing games. I graduated from the University of Pennsylvania with a medical degree and I'm on my way to help my uncle with his office in

Texas." Sophie's voice grew stronger with each word.

"That's quite the story miss." The outlaw grabbed Sophie by the arm. "All right, since no one else is speakin' up I guess you're the lucky one. You better be good, cause the boss don't like disappointment." The man pulled her down the aisle toward the door. Sophie's mother yelled. "Bring her back here!"

The man hurried Sophie down the steps. Her father brought her medical bag and handed it to her. "Don't hurt my daughter." He starred at the outlaw grasping her arm.

The gunman pulled Sophie toward the man on the ground. Blood seeped through his shirt and puddled in the dirt. It didn't look good.

An outlaw got off his horse and walked toward them. "Why did you bring this woman out here?"

"She claims to be a doctor, on her way to Texas. No one else spoke up. She's all we have."

Sophie went to remove the handkerchief over the injured man's face.

"Don't touch that, if you want to get back on the train." The outlaw above her shouted.

"I need to listen to his breathing." Sophie pulled her shaking hand back. She assumed he must be the gang leader.

"You'll have to do it through the bandana."

Sophie's hands trembled as she unbuttoned the man's shirt. She could barely push the buttons back through the holes. Sophie took a few deep breaths to calm herself. She had to gain control of her emotions and concentrate on what needed to be done. Blood pooled around her fingers, she knew this man's life was flowing out before her.

Sophie pulled his shirt apart and discovered that the bullet wound was on the upper right side of his chest. She breathed a sigh of relief as she put pressure on the hole to stop the bleeding. "Would someone roll him on his side so I can see if the bullet passed through?"

The two outlaws next to her rolled him onto his side. The back of his shirt was covered with blood and dirt, she saw the exit wound. "It looks like the bullet passed straight through and missed his lungs, which, thank God, is good news." Sophie took pre-cut bandages out of her bag and placed them over the back hole.

"I don't believe in God." The gang leader snarled.

"It might help you if you did." The words escaped Sophie's mouth before she thought about the wisdom in saying it. She dared a quick glance up. The outlaw didn't smile. "Does anyone have whiskey?"

"I do." One gunman pulled a flask from under his vest.

Sophie poured it on clean bandages, then on both sides of the wound. The injured man moaned but didn't regain consciousness. She cleaned both wounds with the whiskey-soaked bandages before stitching his chest and back closed. Sophie finished by bandaging the wounds with clean dressings.

She handed the gunman more cloth bandages. "Remove the soiled dressings every day and clean the wound with whiskey-soaked bandages before applying new dressings. I think he'll pull through, but he shouldn't be traveling for a few days." Sophie gave a bottle to the man. "If he runs a fever, you'll need to put a small amount of this in tea or water and have him drink it twice a day."

"Why wouldn't I take you with us to look after him?" The leader knelt next to her. "It could be fun having a pretty doctor around to treat our aches and pains." He laughed.

"You said I could go back to my family if I didn't take off his bandana. I could've stayed silent and not helped. You would've never guessed I'm a doctor. I've done all I could to save him." Sophie looked into the dark brown eyes of the stranger. A shiver ran down her back as her confidence slipped. This man couldn't care less if he kept his word.

"You sound pretty sure of yourself. I've killed men just because I wanted to, but lucky for you I've never made a practice of killing women unless they got in my way." He stood up. "You better get back on that train before I change my mind."

Sophie gathered her supplies and closed the bag. She touched the injured man's forehead one last time. It felt cool. "Make sure you give him lots of water."

"Let's get out of here. We're done." The leader motioned for two gunmen to lift the injured man in front of one of the outlaws already on his horse. They galloped away.

Sophie crumpled to the ground as the last of the outlaws faded in the distance.

Her father startled her as he knelt beside her in the dirt. "You are brave. I wish you hadn't put your life at risk. I've never prayed so hard before. If the robber died, it would have served him right. There's a little boy on the train who is injured. He had a bullet graze his arm."

"The robber will pull through if they take care of him. He lost a lot of blood, but the bullet went straight through. I had to give my fear to God or I would've passed out. Father, I've never experienced such evil as when I looked in their leader's eyes. I didn't think he'd let me go." Sophie grabbed her father's hand, and they stood.

"Let's check on the little boy. It was torture watching it all and knowing I couldn't do anything. I understand now why you wanted me to carry a gun, sweetheart. I need to purchase one and ask your uncle to show me how to use it. You should learn too. It's dangerous out west.

Just say the word and we'll go back to Philadelphia. You can live at home until some man sweeps you off your feet. The hospital would love to have you there or I could help you buy an office where you could see patients."

"Father, I can't do that. There are too many doctors in Philadelphia. I need to stay with the plan I've prepared for. Philadelphia is not without danger. We lived where it wasn't as common but it existed. Although, I never feared for my life there. Will the train be able to run?"

"I heard someone say we'll be moving on soon. Thank God they didn't kill the conductor. I don't know how many injuries there are other than the boy. You may be busy."

"What would I do without you, father?"

"Unfortunately, you'll find out when your mother and I head back to Philadelphia. Although, it won't be for a while. No need to dwell on it now."

This morning she hoped to become a doctor. This afternoon she became a doctor but would Nacogdoches be ready for a woman doctor?

She hoped Texas would be more acceptable of a woman doctor. It would be a difficult road ahead, but she felt ready for the challenge. Today she'd been forced into the fire, pulled herself together and relied on her training. There wasn't any reason to expect she couldn't continue doing the same.

She hoped the injured outlaw survived and thought about why he'd been given a second chance. She had prayed for him softly while she stitched his wounds closed and hoped he'd heard.

Chapter Two

Luke saddled his mare. The roan, Duchess, had a stunning blonde mane and dark coat. He hadn't seen many horses like her. Luke loved watching her run. He'd declined many offers from other cowboys wanting to buy or breed her. Luke hoped to have many more years with Duchess.

Luke had worked for Joshua Brown for five years. He liked being a part of his cattle ranch, but lately, he'd been contemplating purchasing a place of his own. Joshua treated him well, but he wanted room for a wife and family.

He'd dreamed about moving to a different part of Texas but he'd miss the friends he'd made here. His job as Joshua's foreman kept him busy and the Brown's welcomed him in as part of their family. They'd been through a lot together.

Three years ago, Anna Wilson, an orphan train agent, had shown up at Joshua's door, threatening to place two of his children with another family. Joshua and his first wife, Sarah, had taken in two children from an earlier orphan train because they hadn't been able to have children of their own. A couple of months later they discovered she was expecting. They had a baby girl, but his wife died from complications in childbirth.

Joshua's sister, Lizzy, came and helped him with the children after his wife passed away. She lived at the ranch for two years until she married. His mother, Clara, then came to take her place, but the burden of taking care of three children, the ranch house, and the garden was too much for her. That's when Anna showed up. Seeing the house and kids in disarray, she had threatened to remove them.

Joshua wouldn't let her take the children from him, instead, he suggested she live at the ranch house and help his mother. He moved out to the bunkhouse. She reluctantly agreed to help until he found someone else and she finished visiting families who had taken in children from past orphan trains. It was part of her job as an agent to visit the families. This gave Clara the support she needed. Anna had a twelve-year-old orphan girl, Ella, with her, they were close. Anna hadn't been able to find a family for her.

Luke entertained thoughts of courting Anna. It didn't take long to realize she and Joshua only had eyes for each other, even though they didn't immediately recognize it. Joshua felt guilty being attracted to another woman besides his late wife, and Anna struggled with memories from a bad relationship. Her employer had seduced her. He then turned his back on her for another woman. She was tossed out on the streets of New York with nothing until she found the job at the orphanage.

While Anna lived at the ranch, she called on a family who had taken in two orphan brothers. During her visits, she suspected the children were being abused, so she tried to get them out of the home. The husband, Henry Weaver, refused to let her take them. He tried shooting her but missed. She was thrown from the wagon and no one found any evidence on who shot at her.

A few weeks later one of the boys fled to a nearby farm and said his brother was missing. They found him beaten and tied to a tree. They finally had evidence Weaver was an evil man, but he got away.

Anna planned on returning to the orphanage and needed to make a trip into town. Luke had Ben, one of the ranch hands, go with her. Weaver intercepted them on the road into town and shot and killed Ben and kidnapped Anna.

Weaver took Anna to a cave in the mountains where he beat and tried to rape her. She grabbed one of Weaver's knives and stabbed him in the throat. He shot her in the arm as she escaped.

Joshua later found Anna unconscious where she'd fallen next to Weaver's horse. Weaver died from the stab wound. He had been as evil as they came. No one shed a tear when he met his maker, although, everyone was shocked such a small woman sent him there. Almost losing Anna opened Joshua's eyes to the fact he loved her, and they married.

Luke heard Joshua and Anna get into a few quarrels over the last three years as they were hard-headed. It didn't take them long to make up though, because they took their promise to each other with all their hearts.

They'd have their first baby in a few weeks. It would be a busy home with five children to love. Luke hoped they'd have a boy but a little girl would be fun too. He always had time for tea parties but showing them the new baby animals was the best. Their eyes glistened in wonderment as they gazed at the little ones.

Because of all that transpired, Joshua and Anna knew they needed a temporary home for children who were left without any relatives. They just completed a two-story home on the property for this purpose. They asked Ben's sister, Megan, if she'd be interested in helping with it. Anna had her hands full with the children and a baby on the way. She could help, but wouldn't be able to do it on her own.

A local family, Bill and Beth Carson, took in the brother's who had been abused by Weaver. Noah and Jack were thriving with their new parents. It made everyone's heart happy to see them doing so well. They'd had a hard life, losing their real parents at an early age, becoming orphans and then almost killed in Weaver's care. Weaver had hurt his wife too, so she was scared to say anything involving her husband.

Ella was fifteen now. Luke couldn't believe how the girl had blossomed in Joshua and Anna's care. She would be a beauty in a couple of years. Joshua would have to keep his shotgun close by. She had a heart of gold and was too pretty for men not to notice.

Ella loved horses and Luke never tired of watching her with them. She was the little sister he never had. The ranch hands treated her with the utmost respect and he pitied the poor guy who tried to court her. She had more protectors than you could shake a stick at.

Ella had been a big help to Anna and Clara with the kids and now that Anna was pregnant she had stepped up. She loved children, and they loved her right back.

"Hey boss, I thought you were riding to town. All you're doing is daydreaming." Steven slapped Luke on the back.

"Yeah, well, that's what happens when you think about the past. You lose all track of time and before you know it half the day's went by." Luke mounted his horse, Duchess. "I'll see you all in a few hours since you're in a hurry to see me leave."

"No hurry boss, just wondering what had you lost in thought."

"Just thinking about all the trouble Weaver gave us three years ago. Glad that man is dead."

Steven stepped away from Luke's horse. "I heard Ben's sister is moving here once Mrs. Brown has her baby. She will help run the home for the orphans. Miss Anderson helped Mrs. Brown after her brother was killed. She left because her mother got sick. Her mother is better, so she's planning on living here, well, at least until she finds a husband. You know how that goes. Once the men get a look at her, they'll be considering getting married and having a ranch of their own. All of them accept me. I don't want a wife. They're too much trouble."

Luke patted Duchess on the neck. "I don't remember a lot about her. That was a crazy time for everyone and she wasn't that old, maybe seventeen. We all felt bad for her. When Weaver shot Ben and kidnapped Anna, we'd hoped Ben would pull through. He was a great kid and you could tell she loved her brother. I'm glad she didn't hold it against any of us."

Steven grabbed a shovel that had fallen to the ground and leaned it against the barn. "Well, none of us thought Weaver was dumb enough to stay around when he was wanted for almost killing one of the boys in his care. His hatred for Mrs. Brown outweighed his smarts."

"Yeah, when someone is bent on revenge you shouldn't put anything past them. We learned our lesson, sadly, too late to help Ben. Even if Mrs. Brown hadn't needed to go into town, Weaver would have devised a plot to get to her a different day. Others could've been killed then as well.

"Weaver rode up on them out of the woods and Ben didn't see him in time. As I said earlier, I'm glad the monster is dead." Luke took his cowboy hat off and wiped his forehead with his bandana. "I better get going or I will not make it to town today."

"See you tonight. If you're not here in time for dinner, I can't promise there will be anything left. You know how these men eat."

"I'll probably eat in town. I haven't eaten at Milly's Restaurant for a while. I love her biscuits and gravy. She makes the biggest biscuits I've ever seen." Luke kicked his horse in the side and they galloped down the road leaving a trail of dust.

~

Luke walked into Milly's. It was crowded tonight. He didn't see an open table, so he might have to wait. The special of the day was roast beef and potatoes. Sounded good, but he'd made his mind up before he left the ranch with the biscuits and gravy.

Hank, the bunkhouse cook, made good food but it couldn't measure up to Clara and Anna's home cooking. He ate dinner with them at least once a week. The second best place he'd found to eat was Milly's.

"Hi, there Luke. I have a table in the back corner if that'll work unless you want to wait. Is it just you?" Milly winked at him.

"You know me, Milly. Too ornery for anyone to accompany me anywhere."

"I remember you bringing a certain school teacher here. What happened, did she go blind? Can't believe a good looking man like you is still single. One of these days, the women around here will open their eyes and snatch you up. If I was twenty years younger, you'd be mine." Milly smiled. Her gray hair had long since left the constraints of the bun it had been pinned into and fell down in tight curls.

"You wouldn't have to snatch me up, Milly. You could've reeled me in with the smells coming from your kitchen. I couldn't have resisted." Luke followed Milly to the table. "Have you heard from those children of yours?"

"Yes, I have. Got a letter from them two days ago. They're all doing great. In fact, there will be a new grandbaby born later this year. I might take time off and visit." Milly gave him the menu.

"I don't need it, Milly. I've been drooling over the prospect of eating your biscuits and gravy all day. Can I get an extra biscuit too?" Luke sat in the wooden chair.

"Of course you can. I'll bring some jam. Gotta take care of my favorite cowboy."

"I need to come here more often, you treat me too good. You should go see your son and his family. You can find someone to run the place while you're gone." Luke set back in the chair tipping it on the back two legs.

"I probably will go visit them. Let me get your order going. Did you want coffee or water?"

"Coffee please." Luke glanced around the restaurant while Milly went to get his coffee.

He saw a young woman sitting with who he believed to be her parents. Luke couldn't remember ever seeing them before. He wondered if they were visiting or moving here. The lady was pretty. Her brown hair fell in loose curls halfway down her back. When she looked his way, her hazel eyes caught his attention, they were unusual.

Milly sat his coffee on the table.

"Milly, do you know who the older couple and the young woman are at the table near the window?"

"I believe they're related to Doc. Not sure why they're here. If they're still here when you're done, would you like me to introduce you?"

"That's okay. I just wondered if they were visiting or staying."

The bell on the door jingled as four men walked in. "Well, gotta go Luke. I guess today is gonna keep me hopping."

"Been good talking to you, Milly. Take care of your customers. I'll probably see them at some town function if they're visiting Doc. I'll try not to be a stranger."

"I'm holding you to your word. Your food should be here soon." Milly walked over and greeted the four men.

The biscuits and gravy filled him up, and Luke needed to head back to the ranch. It could be dark by the time he got there. If the moon was full, riding at night could be interesting, but it looked cloudy through the window and he didn't want to chance riding in the dark. Duchess could step in a hole and break her leg.

When had he gotten so city-fied? He used to ride through the night and sleep outside under the stars with his saddle as a pillow. He was younger then. That must be the reason it no longer appealed to him. He looked forward to the day he could go home to a wife and kids. Time didn't wait until someone had the ideal person or the biggest ranch or the best circumstances, it kept going by and he needed to make plans.

He wouldn't mind if it included a woman like the one by the window. Maybe he should come to town on his days off. Chances were she was visiting and could leave in a week or two.

Luke left a couple of coins on the table and put his hat on. As he stood to leave, the couple and the young woman did too. He timed his steps to walk out behind them so he could hear what they might be saying.

"It looks like we'll need to find a hotel. Your brother doesn't have a big enough place for all of us, Charlotte. I thought he added on to his little space." The man said.

"You're right. I had been under the impression he built more rooms on but he only has the living area and two bedrooms. Staying at a hotel will give us a chance to meet the people who live here. It will help me feel better leaving our Sophie here with my brother." The older woman rubbed the younger woman's back.

"That's a good way to look at it. A month isn't a long time for us to meet the townspeople and if we were staying at your brother's we probably wouldn't see many of them. Let's cross the street and check out the hotel he suggested."

Luke watched them go into the hotel as he mounted Duchess. From what he learned, the young woman named Sophie would be remaining with her uncle after her parents left in a month. He wondered what she might do here. Milly said they were related to Doc Fisher, maybe she had studied to become a nurse. He could use the help since the town continued to grow.

Time to get going, he had an hour ride ahead. He smacked Duchess on the side and they galloped down the street. Thoughts of Sophie's beautiful hazel eyes and pretty face kept him smiling all the way back to the ranch.

Chapter Three

Sophie sat in Uncle Jared's office. He'd left earlier on a house call. She liked talking with him yesterday. The last time her uncle visited Pennsylvania she'd been twelve. He'd filled her head with tales of Texas. He wanted to help people and being a doctor reinforced his belief that life was the greatest gift of all.

His words stirred Sophie's heart, and she wanted to make a difference every day like he did. She completed high school at an all-girls boarding school and later was admitted at the University of Pennsylvania. She earned her medical degree after three years of study and headed west where the demand for doctors was greater.

Her uncle had written to her expressing his concerns of keeping up with the demands of a remote doctor. He hoped Sophie would take over for him. At first, Sophie's parents didn't like the notion of her moving to Texas. As time went by, they agreed it might be best to support her in going so she'd gain experience as a doctor.

The office door flung open and a woman carrying a

baby rushed in. “Help me, my baby is scarcely breathing!”

Sophie ran to the woman and grabbed the baby. “What happened?”

“I’m not sure. I heard him choking and found his sister next to his cradle. When I picked him up, he was gasping for breath. Please help him!”

Sophie turned the baby face down on her forearm, struck the baby’s back a few times and a small ball flew out of his mouth.

“Oh my, his sister must have put that in his mouth.” The mother broke down.

Sophie turned the baby over and he was breathing normally. “It’s not unusual for little ones to pretend to feed their younger siblings. Keep small objects away from them. He’ll be fine now. Luckily small amounts of air made it past the ball.”

“Thank you so much. I wouldn’t have forgiven myself if something happened to him.” The woman left the office hugging her baby tight.

Sophie wondered where the woman’s other children were. Maybe an older sibling stayed with them. It was a good thing she’d been there or the baby might not have made it.

Sophie sat down and breathed a sigh of relief. Now she understood what her uncle had been saying. All the hours of studying had been worth saving one life. It didn’t matter no one had witnessed it. What mattered is, the baby would be fine.

Sophie waited for Mary Leland to stop by. Mary and another woman were agents for the Children’s Aid Society. The orphanage sent abandoned children out west to find suitable homes. The other woman had went back to New York City right after they'd arrived in Nacogdoches. Mary remained behind to care for, Patrick Benson and Katie Johnson. Patrick's arm had been grazed by a bullet during the train robbery.

Sophie wanted to make sure infection hadn't set in the wound. It'd been a traumatic experience for the children and one she would never forget.

The door opened. Miss Leland and the children walked in.

"Hello, Doctor Knowles. Thank you for seeing us today." Mary ushered the children over to Sophie.

"I'm glad you came. Let's look at the wound to see how it's healing. Patrick, would you take your shirt off?" Sophie smiled at the little boy.

Patrick glanced at Miss Leland and when she nodded, he unbuttoned his shirt. Sophie removed the bandage and examined the wound.

"It's healing nicely. As long as you keep it clean it should be better in no time. How long will you all be staying?"

"I'm not certain. There's a former orphan train agent, Mrs. Brown, residing on a ranch outside of Nacogdoches who's opening a home for orphans. I want to talk with her. She might know someone who would take in Patrick and Katie. They don't want to go back to the orphanage.

I've considering asking, Mrs. Brown if she needed help with her endeavor. I enjoy working with children, but not the endless hours on trains or parading the children in front of everyone. I care about the children and it's hard to let them go to families I know nothing about." Miss Leland helped Patrick put his shirt back on.

"I understand. It sounds like it might be a positive change for you. You have experience with children so it would make sense they'd hire you. Patrick and Katie could stay there until they found families. I hope it works out for you and drop by when you can. I'd love to visit more. If anything changes with Patrick's wound please let me check it." Sophie walked them to the door.

"We will Doctor Knowles, and if I get a job, I'll tell you." Mary hugged Sophie. "I appreciate all you've done for Patrick."

~

Sophie helped Uncle Jared take his coat off, it had been raining and he was soaked. "I wondered if you were going to make it back before dark."

"I worry about you, Sophie. I realize I prodded you to come here, but when I think about you on a house call after dark, I'm not positive I should've. Texas is not safe, especially for a woman alone. You should only see patients in the office unless we find a trustworthy man who would travel with you when I can't." Her uncle sat at his desk.

"I've been thinking about that too, Uncle Jared. Although, how would I say no to someone who needs a doctor? I'd insist whoever came for me would have to take me to the person needing aid and I would either stay at their home until morning or they'd ride back to town with me. It makes it harder, but I don't want to be out there alone at night. I'm not familiar with this area or how to stay safe."

Uncle Jared poured himself a cup of coffee. "We'll have to give it a lot of thought. For now, stay here and I will do the house calls. How did things go today?"

"I rescued a baby from choking and examined Patrick's wound. He's the little boy from the train. There wasn't any sign of infection." Sophie pulled the lace shawl tighter around her shoulders. The rain made the temperature fall.

"I'm glad you were here for the baby. Some days I don't have anyone come in and other days it's one patient after another. I've wondered what takes place when I'm gone on a call. Guess I'll learn now that you're here. What did your parents do today? I wish they'd stay. I'd love having my sister near."

Sophie nodded, "I agree. I want them to stay but mother isn't used to the primitive conditions. Father would like it for a time, he loves a good adventure."

"Yes, your mother's a bit spoiled. It takes a strong woman to last out here. You must've inherited your father's courageous spirit."

"I suppose we'll find out." Sophie smiled.

The front door to the clinic swung wide as the bell jingled.

"Doc, are you here?"

"I'm in my office, what's the problem?"

"My gut is hurting something dreadful." A tall dark haired man entered the office and then stopped in his tracks, his face turned bright pink. "I'm sorry, I should've asked if I could come back. I didn't realize you had someone with you."

"You're fine Deputy Samuel. This is my niece, Doctor Sophie Knowles. She just finished her medical degree and is now a licensed doctor. She'll be working with me. There's a good chance she'll be examining you if I'm out on a house call. What did you eat today?"

"A woman doctor. Well, that's a first." Deputy Samuel held out his hand. "Nice to meet you, Doctor Knowles. I had chili at Milly's today with lots of jalapenos, haven't eaten much else."

Sophie shook his hand. "It's probably from eating too much spice. Drink some milk and it should help. If you're not better tomorrow come back in."

Doc Fisher turned to his niece. "Well, let's find your parents and have some supper. It's been a long day and I'm ready to enjoy some good company. If you weren't feeling poorly deputy, I'd ask you to join us. Don't eat any more food today and get some sleep. You're not on duty tonight are you?"

"Not tonight. I finished up for the day. Sherriff Allen will be keeping an eye on things tonight. Thanks for the suggestions. Hope y'all have a delightful evening and stay away from the jalapenos." Deputy Samuel smiled at Sophie.

Sophie stood. "It was nice to meet you, Deputy Samuel. Hope you're better soon."

"I'll see you around. This town is pretty small. Thanks."

"Good Night Deputy." Doc Fisher opened the front door.

They walked in silence across the street to a restaurant on the first floor of the hotel where Sophie stayed with her parents. A fire burned in the marble fireplace inside the hotel lobby. Wood banisters curved along the winding staircase to the upper floors. Royal blue curtains covered the windows and the cushions on the chairs wore the same color.

They liked the food at Milly's, but this restaurant was quieter and her mother preferred it. Charlotte complained about the absence of entertainment in the town. She didn't understand why Sophie would choose to live here.

Sophie didn't mind not having much to do. She'd be so tired most days she wouldn't care. A soft mattress and a warm quilt would be all she needed. She thought her parents should've had more than one daughter so her sister could've been more like their mother. They had wanted other children, but it never happened.

Sophie hadn't been close to her mother because they had nothing in common. Sophie loved her, but when her mother went back to Philadelphia she'd be busy with her friends and events. She'd hardly miss her. Maybe if Sophie had children it would change.

When Sophie turned fourteen and didn't show an interest in her mother's likes, Charlotte started spending more time with friends at teas and events. Sophie hadn't cared, it allowed her time to work on her schooling and pour through medical books. Her father had always been proud of her.

It had been hard becoming a woman doctor. Getting through college had simply been the beginning, now Sophie had to prove herself. She wondered how many people in this small town would welcome her.

She'd noticed a look of hesitation on the women's face who came in with her baby but there hadn't been anyone else. Deputy Samuel had been caught off guard and remarked about the scarcity of women doctors. Word traveled fast in small towns, and she'd soon learn what everyone thought.

"There you are, dear. I'm sure you're famished. What did you do today?" Charlotte sipped her water. "Your father and I strolled along a charming lake and fed the ducks."

"Nothing much, Mother. I saved a baby from choking and checked Patrick's wound, he's the little boy from the train. It's healing nicely." Sophie sat next to her father "I'm glad you enjoyed yourself. I'm sure you're counting the days until you travel home."

"Oh my Sophie, how wonderful! I'm so proud of you. Yes, I'll be happy to get home, but I'll miss you dreadfully. We have lots of time left so let's prolong the goodbyes for as long as possible." Charlotte grabbed Charles' hand.

"We'll be leaving half our hearts here with our daughter, it'll be tough." Charles smiled at Sophie. "Please take every precaution to be safe. I don't want you making house calls like your Uncle Jared. It wouldn't be prudent."

"Uncle Jared and I were just talking about that before we met you for dinner and he expressed the same worries. I'll miss you both too. You'll be so far away. After I get experience as a doctor, maybe I'll move back to Philadelphia or you'll move here." Sophie smiled at her parents.

"Instead of speaking about what might happen let's order dinner. I haven't eaten today and I'm starved." Uncle Jared motioned the server over.

"I'm sorry Jared, we've been going on and on and not even considering you. The special is chicken and dumplings with homemade rolls and salad. I'm going to order that." Charlotte dabbed at the corner of her eye with her napkin.

Could it be a tear? Sophie had never seen her mother cry. She ordered her food and listened to her uncle and parents talk. Her mother might miss her more than she'd anticipated. She'd looked upset when they were talking about it.

Sophie realized she'd be growing up quick and it might get uncomfortable. If she failed, home was a long train ride away. She prayed God would be with her through all that might take place.

Sophie needed to visit the dressmaker tomorrow. Philadelphia fashions were decidedly different from what everyone wore here. She needed dresses appropriate for a doctor. She'd keep her elegant dresses for special occasions or perhaps church on Sunday.

She hadn't noticed what churches were here. Maybe her parents would look tomorrow. She needed encouragement from God's word and His people.

"Sophie, what happened to that little baby today? I failed to ask you." Charlotte buttered a roll and sat it on the plate in front of her. "The mother must've been very glad you were there."

"I don't think she was at first, but when he coughed up the ball and recovered, I think she was. I'm glad I knew what to do."

"Sophie, you've been given a gift and we can't wait to see how it's used. You've blessed our lives and now it's time for you to bless others." Charles put his arm around his daughter's shoulders and pulled her close. "I love you."

"I love you too, Father."

Chapter Four

"How's it going boss?" Luke asked as Joshua walked into the barn. Luke heard Anna was in labor.

"It's been a busy morning. Anna should have the baby today. Would you send someone for Doc? I want him here. I'm trying not to worry but fear is powerful. When your first wife dies in childbirth, you don't want it to happen again. God is with us, but…" Joshua ran his hand through his hair. "… I'm struggling."

"I'll get Doc myself. Most everything is done."

"Thank you, Luke. I'd be lost without your help. After Jim left, you've had to do twice as much. I wish Jim would've talked to me before he took off. We might have been able to work through whatever troubles he had. I need another cattle foreman, but I'm uncertain of who I can depend on.

"Relax, Joshua. I'll talk with the men and find out who they look up to. With Anna about to have a baby, you need to stay here. Are the children helping?"

"Ella is always a help. I don't know what we did to deserve her, but that adopted daughter of mine is pure gold. Her love for Anna and vice versa couldn't be stronger if she'd been her own. Seth and Rebecca are upset as they remember Sarah dying after Emily's birth. It had been a dark time for all of us. Emily's excited she won't be the baby anymore. Our family is made up of children who may not have been born to us but my love for them couldn't be greater. Well, I better get home, so you can find Doc. Thanks again, Luke."

~

Luke tied his horse to the hitching post outside Doc Fisher's office. Main Street was quiet. Only a few horses stood in front of different businesses. The sun warmed the cool morning air enticing everyone to stay home and work their ranches. Tomorrow would be the first of March and he was glad the trees and flowers would bloom soon casting off the dreariness of winter.

"Doc, are you here?" Luke hollered as he strode into an empty office.

"Can I help you?" A female voice yelled from the back.

"Is Doc Fisher here?"

A woman walked into the office. It was Sophie, the woman he'd seen with her parents at Milly's a couple of weeks ago. He couldn't forget her pretty face.

"I'm not Doc, but I'm his niece. My name is Doctor Sophie Knowles and I'll be helping my uncle. I graduated from the University of Pennsylvania with a medical degree. Can I help you?"

Shocked, Luke couldn't speak for a few seconds. *A woman doctor? Since when did they allow women to become doctors?* He'd never heard of such a thing. "My name's Luke Nelson, and I was hoping to find Doc Fisher? When will he be back?"

"He won't be back until late tonight or tomorrow. He had an emergency house call a few miles away. I assure you I'm a doctor and qualified to talk to you about what is wrong." Sophie walked closer to Luke. "I may be a woman, but I've studied and passed my exams just like any man would've."

"All right Doctor Knowles, I'm not trying to be disrespectful. I suppose you'll do. Uh, I mean... you'll do fine. I'm the foreman at the Brown's ranch and Mrs. Brown is in labor. My boss, Joshua Brown, lost his first wife in childbirth and he'd feel better if Doc... you'd be there in case she had any problems. Joshua's mother, Clara, is helping but she's not a nurse or a doctor."

"Mr. Nelson, I'm not sure whether to be offended or flattered you're allowing me to go with you. The dilemma is my uncle doesn't want me to travel alone or after dark."

"You can come with me and if it gets dark, you'll stay with the Browns. Is there a buggy you'd like me to get hitched?" Luke looked down at the spunky woman. He hoped he wasn't making a mistake, and she knew as much as Doc.

"The livery will ready a horse and buggy. I'll leave my uncle a note, grab my medical bag and tell my parents. You can pick me up across the street if that's suitable?"

"I can do that, Doctor Knowles."

Luke hurried to the livery where they hitched up a buggy for him. He stopped in front of the hotel, he'd tied Duchess to the back of the buggy. It wasn't long before Doctor Knowles came out with her father, who helped her in.

Charles introduced himself and shook Luke's hand.

"Mr. Nelson, Please keep an eye on our daughter. It isn't easy letting her make house calls but as a doctor, it's part of her job."

"I will, Mr. Knowles. The Browns are one of the best families around and she'll be fine. I've been a foreman on their ranch for over five years." Luke smiled.

"Thank you, Mr. Nelson. We'll be praying for a safe and quick delivery of the new baby. See you when you return Sophie."

"Thanks, father." Sophie sat her medical bag in her lap.

Luke flicked the reins, clicked his tongue, and they headed out.

"Have you done many baby deliveries, Doctor Knowles?" Luke asked.

"I worked in a large hospital in Philadelphia so I watched and attended many deliveries. This will be my first birth in a home. Has Mr. Brown's mother delivered other babies?"

"I believe so. I've helped cows, horses, dogs, and cats, does that count?" Luke took a long look at Sophie. She was even prettier close-up.

"In an emergency, you'd have a general idea of how it should work. I hope I'll get time to prepare everything before her labor progresses too far."

"It will take us about an hour to get to the ranch. When I left, Joshua didn't act like he expected it would be soon."

Sophie talked about the role of a doctor in labor and childbirth, and while Luke tried to pay attention, he found his mind wandering. Doctor Knowles used medical terms he didn't recognize. He caught himself daydreaming, looking at the surrounding scenery, and doubted if she even noticed.

Sophie remarked how charming the ranch house appeared as they got close. She hadn't expected such a big house. When she thought of ranch houses in the country, she envisioned they'd be small. Luke pulled the buggy up to the hitching post. Before he could help Sophie, she'd gotten out.

An older woman waited on the front porch. "Weren't you suppose to get Doc Fisher, Luke?"

"I did." Luke made the introductions.

"It's nice to meet you, Doctor Knowles. I hope you can help, Anna's contractions stopped, even though her water broke half an hour ago. I don't know what to do? Can't recall ever having this go on before. I'll take you to her room." Clara opened the front door.

"I'll take the horses to the barn and then be back." Luke took the buggy to the barn and walked back to the farmhouse. He let the other men take it in.

Luke walked into the sitting room. The lines in Joshua's face stood out as he paced the floor.

"Joshua, aren't you the one always telling me to not worry because God is taking care of us? Doesn't look like you're trusting Him too much. Has Doctor Knowles said anything yet?" Luke sat in a chair.

Joshua stopped pacing and sat across from Luke. "Not yet, she's still examining her. You're right, but the fears I had when Sarah died have come back. I'm trying to pray through them but it's weighing me down. I can't lose Anna too."

"Where are the children?" Luke leaned forward. "Anna will be fine, this isn't the same as last time."

"They're in the kitchen with Ella, eating a snack. If

you're hungry, I'm sure she'd fix you something. You probably didn't eat today."

Sophie entered the room. "Mr. Brown, Anna is doing great. I'm not sure why her labor slowed, but I want to get her walking around the house. Walking can get the labor going again.

I assume the two of you will go outside until she's back in her room. Mr. Brown, if you like, you can be with Anna during the delivery. It may give you peace being there. Most people consider it inappropriate, but I believe it helps the mother to have her husband's encouragement. If you aren't comfortable being there, I understand."

Joshua stood. "When it gets closer, I'd like to come in but I don't want to annoy her with my pacing. Luke and I will go to the kitchen. He hasn't eaten all day, so he is hungry. Can we get you anything?"

"Maybe a cup of water for Anna and myself. I'll tell you when we're close to the baby's arrival."

~

"Mr. Brown, would you'd like to come in now?" Doctor Knowles stood next to Joshua's chair.

Luke opened his eyes, he'd fallen asleep on the settee and by the looks of it, Joshua fell asleep in the chair.

"Yes, sure, sorry. I must've fallen asleep. I'll be right in."

Doctor Knowles went back in with Anna. Joshua glanced at Luke. "Next time I see you I expect to be holding a baby in my arms."

"Good Luck. Can't wait to meet him or her. I'll check on the horses and then be back."

"Thanks, Luke, you're a good friend."

Luke went through the barn checking in each stall. Everything was in order, the ranch hands managed without him. He wondered if he would ever be a father. Watching Joshua and Anna the last few months made him recognize what he was missing. It'd never bothered him much before, but he was changing. He wanted to talk to Joshua about buying land. Having a home might entice a woman to take him seriously.

Luke wandered over to the corral. He watched Duchess running through the pasture. Life had treated him well. There had always been food to eat and a place to sleep. He had a job where he could work with animals all day. Nothing stirred his soul like saddling a horse and letting it race across an open field. He felt as if he was flying, the horse's hooves barely touching the earth.

Horses would run until they collapsed if you urged them to. Luke ran a horse, one time, so far it fell over. When he pulled the trigger to put his horse out of its misery, his heart broke. He'd misused the trust the horse had given him.

He now harbored anger against anyone who mistreated their animals. If a person hurt animals, then they'd do the same to people. Henry Weaver had been a prime example. The world was a better place without him.

If God cared about everyone, He should've stopped him. Although, it gave Luke satisfaction to imagine him in hell. No man should kill someone unless their life was being threatened. Ben had been a good friend, and Luke missed him. Yep, Weaver deserved every agonizing moment in hell. Eternity wouldn't be long enough.

Chapter Five

"It's a boy." Sophie wrapped the baby in a blanket and handed him to Anna. "Do you have a name picked out?"

"Isn't he handsome, Joshua?" Anna held the baby close as Joshua bent over them.

Tears ran down his face. "You both are." Joshua kissed Anna and his son.

Tears escaped Anna's eyes as she snuggled her baby. "What a miracle he is! All children are miracles but when you have your own, the experience is indescribable. We settled on the name, James William if we had a boy. William was Joshua's father's name."

"I love it. He's a fighter. The delivery was more difficult than most, but you both came through like champions. Thank you for following my directions and walking even though it hurt.

Thank you too, Mr. Brown. Having you in here gave Anna the support she needed. Most men wouldn't have. In my opinion, husbands should understand what mothers go through and witness the miracle of childbirth." Sophie got up to wash her hands. "Childbirth is not for the faint of heart, but if you can handle it, nothing compares to watching the birth of your child."

"Thank you, Doctor Knowles, Your uncle knew what he was doing when he suggested you come to Nacogdoches. Now we're blessed with two great doctors." Anna kissed her son's forehead.

"Thank you for trusting me. A woman doctor is not an accepted occupation." Sophie dried her hands. "Anna, let's get that little guy nursing. If you want to tell everyone the news, Joshua, now would be a good time. Once I get Mother and baby cleaned up and James eats, they can come see him. Could you ask your mother if she would help me?"

~

Ella scooped scrambled eggs onto her plate. "Doctor Knowles, how did you become a doctor?"

"Sophie sipped her tea. First, I completed my schooling at the boarding school I attended. Then I applied for the University of Pennsylvania and they accepted me. I studied there for three years and helped in a local hospital until I graduated with my medical degree."

"I never realized there were women doctors until you came here. It's exciting to think I can be so many things. I wouldn't choose to move and settle so far away to go to a university. I waited so long to have a family, I'm not ready to give them up. We have a new baby brother and I'd planned on helping mother with the home for orphans." Ella scooped oatmeal onto Emily's plate.

"Whatever you chose Ella, you'll do it wonderfully. You have a big heart and are eager to learn. You're devoted to those you love and always help." Sophie took a bite of biscuit. “This is delicious, Clara, you’re an excellent cook. Thank you for letting me stay last night.”

“Will father and mother come out soon?” Rebecca asked.

“They’re both tired, they may sleep most of the day. Your father and mother are blessed to have a family who loves them so much.”

“I’ve heard there are new puppies around here someplace.” Sophie smiled at the children. “Would one of you show them to me?”

“Oh, we’d all love to show you.” Seth jumped down from his chair.

“Let’s give everyone a chance to finish their food and then we’ll go.” Sophie winked at Clara.

Luke soaked up the last of his gravy with a biscuit. “Well, since I’ve not done any chores yet, I should check on the animals. Find me when you go out to the barn and I’ll help round up those puppies. The food was delicious, Clara.” Luke stood up.

“Aren’t you going to eat a cinnamon roll?” Clara gathered up the dirty plates.

“I can’t eat another bite. I’m sure Seth won’t mind eating mine.”

“Luke’s right about that, grandma. I’d love to have two.” Seth took the dishes to the kitchen.

“You don’t know what you’re missing.” Clara sat two pans of cinnamon pecan rolls on the table.

“Oh I do, that’s why I better leave now before I change my mind.” Luke went out the back door.

Sophie took a bite of her pecan roll. The caramel frosting and pecans over the cinnamon roll tasted amazing. She couldn’t recall ever eating anything this good. Her mother never cooked. They hired someone to do their cooking.

What a night it had been. Her first birth by herself. She breathed a prayer of thanks for it turning out so well. She had worried having Anna walk might not get the contractions going again, but it had. It worked out and now they had a beautiful son.

The Browns were a remarkable family. Everyone pitched in and helped each other and they genuinely cared. Children growing up in this family were lucky. The pecan rolls were an added bonus.

Sophie had slept in the bedroom across from Joshua and Anna in case they had any concerns. She wondered if Uncle Jared would be here soon. Sophie hoped he'd be proud of how she managed everything.

Rebecca took hold of Sophie's hand. "Are you ready to see the puppies, Doctor Knowles?"

Sophie left her daydreams for another time. "I am. I can't wait. Let's go get our fill of puppy kisses."

~

Doc Fisher got into the buggy next to his niece. "We're taking a puppy home? Don't you have enough to keep you busy?"

"I do, Uncle Jared, but on nights when you're gone and I'm alone I'll need company? You have to admit she's the cutest."

"I can't disagree with you, she's adorable. Have you settled on a name for her?"

"Yes, her name is Callie."

"Fits her perfectly. I'm confident she'll have us wrapped around her little paw in no time." Doc Fisher urged the horses to go faster. "You did a great job delivering the Brown's baby. Joshua and Anna were grateful you were there with them. You did everything right. Anna and the baby are healthy and happy."

"I worried when her labor ceased, but I had her walk, which caused her contractions to start again. I'm glad Joshua came in with Anna, they helped calm each other's fears. Most men won't stay with their wives but it helps them both."

The puppy fell asleep on Sophie's lap.

"You're right, men won't want to be in there. If you want to give them the choice, it's up to you. I'll stick to the way I've always done it because I don't need the husbands causing issues when I'm helping their wives. You're lucky it was Joshua Brown, he's a good man, and he loves his wife and family. That isn't always the case. I've seen some cruel men, well, and women too." Doc Fisher swatted a fly from in front of his face.

"I can imagine. We dealt with a lot of horrible things in Philadelphia. A doctor's work is not just helping the sick but witnessing what people do to each other. I wish we could all get along, but there's evil in this world and people make bad choices. I saw it first hand when our train was robbed. The gang leader had an angry, vacant stare, and he'd as soon shoot you as let you live. I'm surprised he didn't leave his friend to die and he let me go. I doubted I'd make it back on the train." Sophie petted Callie behind her ears as she slept.

"I can't imagine how scared you and your parents must've been through the whole ordeal. Do you think the robber survived?"

"He had a nasty bullet wound that went straight through his right shoulder. I cleaned it well and got it stitched up. It's hard to say how many miles they traveled, or if they kept him nourished and gave the wound time to heal. I have a suspicion they rode long and hard making sure no one would catch up to them."

"Sounds like his chances were slim, but you did everything you could. Even in the best of circumstances, we lose them. They need to stop the outlaws. If they can't make the trains safer, people won't use them."

Sophie sat back and looked around. The scenery was beautiful and the temperature cool enough that the high Texas humidity wasn't a factor.

Joshua and Anna's little boy was adorable, she couldn't wait to go back and check on him. Luke had been a great help with the children. He wasn't uncomfortable around them and they adored him. He also gave her the cute puppy.

Sophie wondered why he'd never married. He was handsome enough. His blonde hair and blue eyes would make any woman's heart swoon. Mr. Brown relied on him so he must be trustworthy and hard working. It didn't make sense he wasn't courting anyone. Sophie imagined if she was searching for a husband she'd be interested, but she needed to focus on being a good doctor and didn't need distractions.

Her parents would go home in a couple of weeks and it would be hard to say goodbye. The next time she visited them she'd be a different woman. Sophie had to be tough to face everyone's doubts she would be a good doctor. She might gain the women's trust, but the men wouldn't want her near them if they had a choice.

Sophie had been spoiled growing up. Her father's job afforded them the finest of everything and being an only child made her the focus of attention. Her room was bigger than her uncle's whole house, which was the back part of his office. There wouldn't be any shops here to buy the latest fashion or events which required her to dress up.

The town buildings came into view and Sophie was ready for a hot bath and a nice long nap. She hadn't slept well because she'd gotten up a few times during the night to check on the baby. Anna would be a natural at being a new mother since she had already mothered so many.

Sophie needed to talk to her father because Callie would need a fence built to keep her in. She doubted she'd be getting a nap in it looked like she'd have to be busy getting Callie settled.

Sophie noticed a man riding toward town. He slumped forward in the saddle, he must be as tired as she felt. Sophie wondered if the guy saw them. He looked intent on getting into town, not glancing around. Why did it matter anyway? People passed through Nacogdoches all the time.

"Well, Sophie, are you ready for some lunch or are you wanting to clean up first?"

Her dress had been blue but turned brown from the dust kicked up by the horses. She'd gauge how bad she looked by her mother's face. "I'll clean up first, but go ahead and eat. I'm not hungry after the big breakfast we had at the Brown's ranch. Those pecan cinnamon rolls were delicious. It would be worth making house calls out there just for the food."

"Oh no, my secret's out. Now you'll be racing me to make sure you're the one going to the house calls at the Brown's."

"You better believe it uncle. Those cinnamon rolls are indeed worth all this dust and that's saying something."

Sophie held Callie and stepped from the buggy with her uncle's assistance. She'd get Callie settled at the office before her bath. Sophie hoped she wouldn't whine too much. She couldn't wait to show Callie to her mother. They'd always wanted a dog but had never persuaded her father.

She found old blankets and laid the puppy in them. Callie snuggled into the soft folds and went back to sleep. Sophie put a water bowl by her. She'd get Callie's food after the bath. The cute little puppy sure was adding a lot more responsibility to her life.

Chapter Six

Wesley galloped past a buggy on Main Street in Nacogdoches. He'd spotted the buggy as they'd both been coming into town at the same time from opposite directions. An older man and a young woman carrying a puppy got out of the buggy and walked inside a building. As he rode by, he read the sign on the building, "Doctor Frasier, M.D."

When Wesley learned his sister, Katie, was on an orphan train headed to Nacogdoches he'd checked at towns along the train's destinations. He arrived at each location a few days behind the train. She had to be here as it was the train's last stop. If she was, he wanted to see if Katie remembered him before he told everyone he was her brother. She had been four and he fifteen when he'd left her at an orphanage in New York City seven years ago.

His parents and two more sisters had died in a fire in their apartment building. They were all very sick with cholera except for Wesley. His parents asked him to find a doctor for Katie. He scoured the city in hopes of finding a doctor who'd look at her without compensation. He'd almost given up when he found a doctor who checked her and immediately admitted her to the local hospital. The doctor told Wesley to bring the rest of his family in and he'd make certain they were taken care of.

When Wesley got back to the apartment building, it was engulfed in flames. The neighbors in the building knew his family was sick, but no one risked their lives to save them. They had their own families to take care of. A wave of guilt hit Wesley so forcefully he had yet to get over it. Logic told him he couldn't be in two places at the same time, but his heart wondered if he'd rushed home as fast as he could have.

Wesley returned to the hospital distraught over the death of his family. The doctor arranged for the hospital to allow him and his one-year-old sister to stay in a hospital room until she recuperated. The doctor contacted an orphanage in New York City and requested they'd take them in after his sister got well.

They lived in the orphanage three years. Wesley had to find work in order to provide for them. He searched for something in the city, but any job he found wouldn't even support himself. Wesley headed west because he heard there was money to be made.

When he reached Texas, he took a job driving cattle and thus began five years of riding the range. He'd made a decent salary, but the days were long and hard. The last couple of years he'd spent his wages wondering from place to place seeking steady work. The rail lines had brought an end to cattle drives as they connected each part of the country. He'd planned to be gone a year or two. That was seven years ago.

Wesley gave up on his dreams of getting wealthy and decided to get his sister and find a job on a ranch. A month ago, he wrote a letter to the orphanage telling them he was headed back to New York to get Katie. They informed him she'd been sent west on an orphan train as they'd given up hope in him returning. The orphanage felt it was the best opportunity for her to find a family.

They gave him a description of how she looked and a list of towns the orphan train stopped at. He had met a couple at the preceding stop that claimed a girl matching her description was still on the train which gave him hope she'd be at the last stop in Nacogdoches.

He needed to find her and make up for the years they'd been apart. He failed his parents by not keeping her with him.

Wesley was hungry. He hadn't eaten since yesterday. He spotted a restaurant called, Milly's, and tied his horse to the hitching post and walked inside. There were only a few customers, so he sat at a table near the window. His thoughts lingered on his sister. He needed to find the orphan train agent. Had his sister found a family or would they send her back to New York City?

A plump middle-aged woman approached him. "Hello, handsome. I'm Milly, the owner of this fine establishment. Are you staying or just passing through Nacogdoches?"

"I'll be here for a few days, ma'am."

"Well, it's good to have you as long as you abide by our laws." Milly smiled and winked at him. "Our special today is beans and dumplings with cornbread and fried potatoes. I have apple or pecan pie for dessert."

"Sounds delicious. I'll have the special, a piece of

apple pie and a cup of coffee. Oh, and a glass of water, please." Wesley sat his cowboy hat on the chair next to him.

"Certainly honey, I'll have it right out." Milly went through the swinging doors into the kitchen.

The older man Wesley had noticed earlier walked into the restaurant and sat a couple of tables away. "You must be new to town, don't believe I've seen you before. I'm Doc Fisher."

Wesley leaned over to shake his hand. "I just rode in and thought I'd eat before I found a place to stay. Not sure how long I'll be here. I'm looking for a job so I've been searchin' from town to town."

"What type of job are you seeking?" Doc Fisher leaned back in his chair.

"I've been driving cattle for about six years. I've taken care of horses too."

"Hmm, you might be a great fit at the Brown ranch. Joshua Brown has one of the biggest cattle ranches around and he's one of the fairest men you'll ever meet. If you treat him right, he'll do the same for you. His cattle foreman quit a few months ago, and he's had a tough time replacing him. They're about an hour from town so you might want to go out and talk with him if you're serious about getting work." Doc Fisher checked the time on his pocket watch.

"I'll do that. It'd be nice to have a steady job. I'm tired of moving from town to town and not finding any work." Wesley took a long drink of water.

"So will it be the usual, Doc?" Milly sashayed over to his table.

Wesley wondered how her broad hips kept from knocking the chairs over as she walked. She must have it timed just right.

"You know me well, Milly. Bacon, eggs, and pancakes are my favorites, any time of day. Can I get a cup of coffee too?"

"It'll be right out. Are your niece and her parents joining you?"

"No, she's eating with her parents tonight at the hotel. She brought a puppy back from the Brown's ranch and has to get it settled at my office before she can go to dinner. I'm afraid I'll be regretting this puppy, as it will more than likely keep me awake all night."

Milly shook her head. "Puppies are good for sleepless nights, not to mention the messes. I don't have time for them but it'd be nice to have the company. Well, I best get y'alls order in and bring your coffee."

Doc Fisher looked back over at Wesley. "Milly has the best food in town. The hotel's restaurant is all right, but I'd rather eat here."

"Sure smells good. My stomach is rumbling in anticipation." Wesley finished off the rest of his water.

It wasn't long till Milly brought out the food and coffee. "If you two gentlemen need anything else holler. I'm going to catch up on some dishes before the supper crowd comes in."

"Don't have any help today?" Doc took a big bite of his pancake.

"My cook and dishwasher didn't show up. It's going to be a long night."

"You need to find more dependable help. You're not getting any younger." Doc slurped his coffee.

"You sure know how to flatter a girl but you said it cause you love me." Milly patted Doc on the back. "I'm thinking of hiring a couple more people. Business is picking up, and I am tired. I'll be back to check on you both in a bit."

Wesley ate his meal in silence. Doc was too busy eating to talk. Once the food hit his stomach, he felt what three days of riding did to one's body. He decided the only other thing he'd do was get a room and sleep. Looking for his sister would have to wait for tomorrow.

He said goodbye to Doc and left his money on the table. The sky to his west was colored in pink and golds. Dusk settled over the streets as he walked to the hotel and got a room.

He wasted no time getting to his room and crawling in bed.

Chapter Seven

A light knock on Sophie's hotel door woke her.

Last night, after getting the puppy settled in a box she'd made, she retired to her room and fell asleep. The excitement of delivering her first baby had left her exhausted. She vaguely recalled her mother peeking into her room to ask if she was meeting them for dinner. She didn't remember answering, just rolling over.

"Who is it?" Sophie yelled.

"It's Melanie from the front desk. Mary Leland left a message for you."

"Could you slide it under the door? I'm just now waking up."

"I'm sorry if I woke you, Doctor Knowles. I worried it might be important and didn't want to wait too long before bringing it. Of course, I can slide it under the door. Hope you have a great day."

"You too and thank you for delivering the letter so promptly."

Sophie tiptoed across the cold floor, snagged the note and jumped back into bed. She tugged the blankets up and read it.

Doctor Knowles,

I wonder if I might meet with you today. I will be eating breakfast with the children at Milly's and then plan on going to the small lake near the white church. If I don't hear from you by the time we're done, I'll stop by Doc Fisher's office.

Thank you, Mary Leland, Orphan Train Agent

Sophie wondered why Mary needed to speak with her. If it had something to do with Patrick's wound, wouldn't she have gone to the office? She got dressed and went down to the restaurant. Her parents were finishing their meal.

"There you are, dear. You must be famished since you missed dinner last night. Have a seat and I'm sure they'll be right over with coffee." Charlotte dabbed her lips with the linen napkin.

Sophie sat next to her father. "I don't have much time, but maybe some coffee and a sweet roll. They do have wonderful cinnamon rolls here."

"You should eat something a little healthier. How about eggs and toast?" Charlotte smiled at her daughter.

"I'll be fine with the cinnamon roll, but thanks mother." Sophie stirred a sugar cube into the coffee the server poured.

"Why are you in such a rush, honey?" Charles patted her hand.

"I need to check Callie and see Miss Leland. She sent me a message asking if she could meet with me. I'm not sure why, but don't want to keep her waiting too long."

"That is puzzling. She might be worried about the little boy who got shot." Her father's brows furrowed as he contemplated the possibilities.

"I considered that, but you'd assume she'd go to the office. It must be something else." Sophie watched the butter run down the sides of the warm cinnamon roll just put in front of her.

Her mother tucked a loose curl back under her hat. "I guess you'll find out soon. Better eat your cinnamon roll while it's warm."

~

The reflection of the steepled church on the lake painted the perfect picture of tranquility. Ducks swam near a group of children on the bank as they threw them breadcrumbs. Sophie didn't see Miss Leland, they must still be eating.

She sat on a bench under a giant oak tree and observed the children. They were giggling and challenging each other to coax a duck over to them. She missed the carefree days of childhood. Running through the grass and playing house with her friends. They'd pretend they were married and had to make dinner, shop and clean their house in the trees. Recess went by quickly and before she anticipated it, the bell rang, signaling it was time to go back to class. Their pretend homes in the trees had to wait until the next day.

"Pardon me, Doctor Knowles, I'm sorry we kept you waiting. Milly's restaurant was busy, and it took longer than I expected." Miss Leland sat next to Sophie and held out a bag to Katie and Patrick. "Why don't the two of you join the other children feeding the ducks?

I'm sorry I asked you to meet me on such short notice. I'm running out of time and can't find anyone to care for Patrick and Anna. I don't want to take them back to the orphanage. They'd be there until they turn sixteen. The Children's Aid Society doesn't send them out on more than one orphan train.

I've spoken to Mrs. Brown about placing them in the home she's opening. The Texas air and sunshine would be much more pleasant than the overcrowded orphanage. The attention Anna gave them would far surpass anything at the orphanage.

She's trying to open it soon and said they'd be welcome there, but it won't be running for a few weeks. I heard she had her baby yesterday, what a blessing. The dilemma is I can't stay that long. Miss Baker, the schoolteacher, said she'd take in Patrick until the home is open. I was hoping you and your uncle might take in Katie for a few weeks? You both are busy but between the two of you, it might work. I've asked everyone else who might be suitable." Miss Leland sat back on the bench. She'd been wringing her hands together as she spoke.

Sophie watched as Katie and Patrick met the other children. They greeted them and explained they were trying to outdo each other in duck coaxing. "Why did Miss Baker choose Patrick instead of Katie?"

"She said she grew up with younger brothers and didn't have any sisters, so she feels more comfortable with Patrick. I didn't argue with her as it's hard to find someone to take them in."

"I understand. I'll have to talk with my uncle before I can give you an answer. There isn't much living area in the back of his office. There's two small bedrooms, a kitchen, and a small sitting area. I'm certain the children will love living with the Browns. Mrs. Brown is so charming. I delivered her adorable baby boy yesterday."

“How exciting for you. They would be well taken care of with the Browns. Mrs. Brown wouldn’t let them leave unless she’d found a great family for them. I wish I could keep them both. They have been such sweethearts and little Patrick was so brave when he was shot.” Miss Leland paused as a chipmunk scurried up the tree. “I can’t thank you enough for taking care of him like you did. I wired the orphanage about it all.”

Sophie noticed a man walking around the other side of the lake. He observed the children and it made her uneasy.

“Do you see the man over there?” Sophie asked.

“I just noticed him. He seems overly interested in the children. I hope he doesn’t mean them any harm. We should walk over and tell them to go home and I’ll take Katie and Patrick back to the hotel.”

“Sounds like a good idea.”

They told the children to leave. Most of them grumbled and didn’t want to until Miss Leland whispered they were worried about the man across the lake. They ran off as he walked toward them. Sophie and Mary tried to get Katie and Patrick away but he caught up with them.

“Where did all the children go?” The man smiled at Sophie. “Did you scare them away?”

“We told them it was getting close to supper time and they should head home.” Sophie avoided eye contact as she spoke the lie.

“I figured you might’ve whispered to them a scary man was headed their way and they should skedaddle. I’m Wesley Johnson and I rode in yesterday hoping to find work here. I promise I’m not as strange as you might expect.” He held his hand out to Sophie.

She shook his hand and glanced up at him. Wesley could outdo any man she'd ever been around in looks. Rugged, bearded and green-gray eyes which pierced right through her defenses. She sputtered. "I'm Doctor Sophie Knowles, my uncle is the town doctor. I'm here to help him. This is Miss Mary Leland, she's an orphan train agent, and this is Katie and Patrick."

"Nice to meet y'all. I've wondered where a good fishing place might be. That's why I was walking around the lake. Didn't notice any jumping but observed how much the children were enjoying feeding the ducks.

A woman doctor? Have never met one before, but I'm sure you must have experience." Wesley hoped Doctor Knowles didn't receive his words the wrong way.

"Women doctors are uncommon but one day we'll be as commonplace as men. I've had the same education as a male doctor so I'm as qualified as they are."

Wesley turned to Miss Leland. "What does an orphan train agent do?"

"I travel with children from the orphanages in New York City out west to find homes for them. In New York, the orphanages are full. They needed a solution which gave the children a chance to find a family. So the Children's Aid Society was organized. The agents are responsible for finding good families for the children. This is our last stop. I'll be heading back after I finish the visits I need to do with all the families that have welcomed children in on previous trains." Miss Leland shooed a bee away.

"Sounds like a serious job. I'm sure the children are

grateful for this chance. How do you know they're going to good families?" Wesley asked.

"When they first started taking the children west, they didn't investigate the families as well as they should have, however, the last couple of years we've done much better. Families now need good recommendations from the town leaders, pastors, and school teachers. I'm sure it's not one hundred percent full proof, but it's better.

In Nacogdoches, there's a retired orphan train agent who is building a home for children who have nowhere to go. I'm hoping Katie and Patrick can live with her. She's wonderful with the children." Miss Leland patted the children on their shoulders.

"Well, I need to go to the restaurant and have some supper. Nice to meet you ladies and I'm certain I'll see you again." Wesley smiled and wandered back toward the street.

"He certainly is a handsome man." Miss Leland blushed.

"I hadn't noticed." Her second lie for the day, she needed to do some serious repenting tonight. She wouldn't admit it out loud, but he was nice to look at. She'd always considered men with dark hair mysterious.

Sophie's life had been busy with school and working at the hospital. She hadn't had time to think about men or marriage. There were guys at the university who had shown interest, but she never encouraged them. She didn't want the distraction.

Sophie needed to let Callie out. She and her uncle were riding out to the Brown's to check on Anna and the baby later.

"I'll consider what you asked and let you know, Miss Leland. I have to visit a patient so I better go. It was nice to see you again."

"Thanks for meeting me. I'll look forward to hearing from you and hope your patient is doing well. Let's go children. Why don't we eat some ice cream?"

Screams of happiness echoed in Sophie's ears as she strolled back to check on her puppy and meet up with her uncle.

When she opened the door to the office, she discovered a man holding a cloth over his arm.

"Where's Doc Fisher? I've been waiting and I'm bleeding."

"I see that sir." A small amount of blood had pooled on the floor. "I'm not sure where Doc is, but I can help you. I'm also a doctor and Doc Fisher is my uncle." Sophie went up to the man to assess the injury.

"I ain't never met no woman pretending to be a doctor. I don't trust you?"

"My uncle, Doc Fisher does, so if you trust him then I hope you will trust me. Right now you have two options. Let me help you, or sit here and bleed to death waiting for my uncle. If you want my help, follow me to the exam room." Sophie didn't look back.

He followed her.

"Please, sit down."

Sophie cleaned and stitched up his wound. "You'll be as good as new in no time. Stop by next week and let my uncle or I take out the stitches. If it becomes red or warm to the touch or you run a temperature, come back in as quickly as possible." Sophie gathered up the soiled instruments and cloths.

"Thank you. For a woman, you done good. What do

I owe you?" The dirty, freckled faced man asked.

"Don't worry about it. I won't charge you as long as you tell all your friends what a good doctor I am." Sophie gave him a roll of gauze.

"I'm not sure they'll believe me, but you gotta deal. They might laugh because a woman treated me, but I don't care. I'm still alive." He stood and grabbed the jacket he'd left on a chair. "See ya next week."

"Remember to come in if it looks red or warm to the touch." Sophie sat in a chair.

Why did everyone question her each time she tried to help them? How could she get anyone to trust and believe she was as competent as her uncle? They weren't going to make it out to the Brown's today. Her uncle must've been called out.

Sophie checked on Callie. She was sound asleep. She'd take her for a walk when she woke up. She decided to find her parents. They'd be leaving soon, and she hadn't spent much time with them. She'd miss them.

When she'd set out on this journey of becoming a doctor, she never dreamt she'd end up in Texas. Sophie assumed she'd work in Philadelphia, but they had enough doctors. Out west, you were lucky if you had more than one doctor in a hundred mile radius.

She was in for an adventure. She prayed it would be a good one.

Chapter Eight

"That little boy is as strong as can be. You look great too Anna, just be careful not to overdo it because you feel better. Your body requires rest and little James needs a healthy mother." Sophie put her stethoscope in the bag. "You have an abundance of responsibilities and it's tempting to get back to them, but right now you need to concentrate on rest and taking care of your baby. Everything else will be there when it's time."

Anna extended her hand to Sophie and grasped hers for a few seconds. "I'm so glad you moved to Nacogdoches. We all love your uncle and he's been so valuable to us, but it's nice to have a woman doctor for delivering babies. Joshua wished to thank you for letting him come in with me." Anna paused to wrap the blanket tighter around James. "He said seeing his child be born was a blessing and something he'd never forget."

"Thanks for telling me, Anna. I hope one day it will be customary for a man to be in with his wife, but I'm sure it won't happen very fast. Sadly, childbirth is still considered something the husband shouldn't see, although husbands have had to deliver their babies in many instances because no one else was around. If I ever have children, I want my husband there to support me and make certain the doctor is doing what they should."

Sophie sat in the chair next to Anna's bed. "Anna, I have something else I'd like to talk to you about. I spoke to Miss Leland yesterday, and she asked me if I would take in Katie until you and Mr. Brown had the home for the orphans ready. I'm not sure we have sufficient room for another person. How long will it be until you're ready to accept children?"

"We've asked, Megan, the sister of one of our former ranch hands to help. My daughter, Ella, will also help, although, since she met you she's talked about nothing other than becoming a doctor.

The interior is done, but we're waiting on furniture to arrive from back east. We need to collect outgrown children's clothes and toys from families around Nacogdoches for the orphans. We also need linens, towels, and other items.

When that comes together, we can let children in. My hope is three to five weeks. You can never predict what might take place, so you hope for the best. I'll be overseeing things, but I have so much to do with the new baby. Sophie, would Miss Leland consider living here and helping?

Joshua and the ranch hands are building homes on the property so the people we hire will have a place to live. It's away from the men's bunkhouse, of course."

"I commend you and your husband, Anna. It's quite an undertaking of love along with your other duties on the ranch. I'll talk to Miss Leland. If she stays, the children would be with her. Sounds like a perfect plan for everyone."

Anna rocked James in her arms while he cooed at the sound of her voice. "One of the homes may be done. I'll have to check with Joshua, but she might be able to move in right away. If Miss Leland agrees, it would be wonderful and an answer to prayer."

"I admire your determination in following through on your dreams, many will be blessed because of it. I'll tell Miss Leland you'd like to talk with her in a couple of days, once you're stronger. Katie and Patrick will love having other children to play with. They're both well-behaved from what I've witnessed."

Anna reached for the glass of water from her bedside table. "Will you ask her to come out Friday afternoon for tea and refreshments? I'll ask Mother to bake her delicious shortbread cookies. I'd love to have you come too, Sophie. I'll have one of the ranch hands pick you all up."

A breeze gently wafted through the white lace curtains at the window. Sophie was grateful for the cool breeze as the room was warm. She heard the children playing outside. They must be chasing Callie and the other puppies around.

"I'd love to come. I'll check on you and little James while I'm here. If something comes up, I'm sure Miss Leland will fill me in when she gets back.

Well, I should go and let the two of you take a nap. Uncle Jared has been outside with Joshua this whole time. He may not be ready to head back since he seldom gets to visit without fretting about working. I'm glad he let me see you without his hoovering." Sophie laughed as she picked up her bag. "I'm certain it's hard for him to not make sure I'm doing it right."

"Thanks again, Sophie. I'm looking forward to Friday. My eyes are getting a little heavy. I suppose you can't fool the doctor." Anna smiled.

"Enjoy your precious little one. Let me know if you have any concerns." Sophie smiled, closed the door behind her and walked out to the sitting room where her uncle, Joshua, and Luke were visiting.

"How are they doing?" Joshua asked.

Sophie sat next to her uncle. "They're both great."

"Good to hear. They had an excellent doctor." Her uncle patted her on the back.

"I'm glad you think so." Heat warmed Sophie's cheeks. "Are you ready to go back to town? If not I'll take a tour and look at the animals."

"Take some time to walk around. I'll visit until you come back."

Luke stood. "Do you need a guide? Our men are harmless, but I can show you the where the animals are. Well, you've seen where the puppies are. They were running outside with Callie and the children?"

"Callie loves coming back here. If you have time, I'm sure you'll keep me from getting in people's way, Mr. Nelson."

"Please, no Mr. Nelson, just Luke. I haven't completed any work today, so why start now?" Luke smiled at Joshua. "I'm glad the boss considers me a hard worker or I might be out of a job."

"I'd be lost without you, Luke. By all means, enjoy your day off." Joshua laughed.

Sophie followed Luke to the barn. She was astonished at how huge it was on the inside. Everywhere she looked there were horses in stalls. Luke led her to a stall at the end of the row. "This is my horse, Duchess."

"She's beautiful."

"Would you like to pet her?"

"Of course, if she won't mind."

"She's great with people." Luke opened the stall door.

Sophie went up to Luke's horse and let her sniff her hand before she patted her on her nose. Duchess enjoyed Sophie's touch. "I love horses."

Luke handed Sophie a sugar cube and stayed behind her while she gave it to Duchess. "I agree, nothing better than a horse."

Sophie felt Luke's breath on the back of her neck, it sent tingles down her spine. She'd never had a man so close to her. It was disconcerting and exciting at the same time. She didn't know what to do.

"She's a bit spoiled. I always carry sugar cubes with me when I come into the stall." Luke rubbed Duchess' nose, bringing his arm around Sophie's side.

"I can see you take good care of her. It says what kind of person you are. If you care for your animals properly, it's likely you do the same with everybody else."

Duchess snorted and tossed her head to the side startling Sophie who stumbled backward toward Luke. Luke put his arms around her to make sure she didn't lose her balance. Sophie regained her balance and turned her head around to thank Luke. They almost bumped noses, she was so close. She drew in a quick breath to calm herself. Her heart raced.

Luke bent forward and Sophie panicked. He meant to kiss her. She stepped away but tripped over the horse's hoof and ended up in the straw on her backside.

When she put her hands behind her to push herself up, they went into something warm and squishy. She squealed, causing Duchess to jump to the other side of the stall. Sophie got up and ran out of the stall to the house.

She'd never been so embarrassed. Her hands were covered in horse poop and she didn't know where she could wash them off. She spotted a rider coming toward the ranch house. She saw a pump by the side of the house and rushed to it as the rider stopped by the hitching post at the front of the house. He hopped down and strode toward her.

Sophie was mortified. It was Wesley, the guy from the lake yesterday. *How could someone so educated end up in a moment like this*?

"Need some help? You got yourself in a bit of a mess." Wesley laughed.

"I'm glad you find it funny. If you don't mind, would you pump the water?" Embarrassed, Sophie glared at Wesley.

"I've got it." Luke walked up and pumped water out. "Wouldn't want to get any horse manure on the pump handle."

Wesley was really laughing now. Sophie was fuming and she could tell Luke was struggling hard not to bust out laughing too. All of a sudden, Sophie let go of the indignation and laughed. Once she started, Luke busted out laughing too.

They got themselves under control after a couple of minutes, and Wesley introduced himself to Luke. He mentioned he'd met Sophie yesterday, and he came out hoping to find a job because he heard they needed someone who was good with cattle.

The front door of the ranch house opened and slammed shut. Her uncle came around the corner. “Are you ready to go home? I need to ride out to the Carson farm to check on, Mrs. Carson, she is due any day. She and Mrs. Brown are good friends and their babies are due a couple of weeks apart.

“Did you need me to come?” Sophie walked around Luke and Wesley to stand by her uncle.

“Goodness Sophie, what is that odor?” Doctor Fisher put his hand over his nose. “The outhouse is over there.”

Wesley and Luke tried not to burst out laughing again.

“Uncle Jared, how could you?” Sophie gave him the, you're embarrassing me look. “I fell in one of the horse stalls. I better go to the hotel and take a bath. I don’t want to meet them smelling like this.” Sophie heard Wesley and Luke still snickering.

“I would hope not. It might send her right into labor. You better get cleaned up before your mother catches a whiff.” Doctor Fisher chuckled and Luke and Wesley busted out laughing again.

“You all are laughing at my distress. If I had a more delicate nature, I probably would’ve fainted from the nastiness of it all. But since I’m used to seeing much worse, I didn’t.” Sophie glanced over at her uncle which made him laugh all the harder.

“You should’ve heard her scream when she realized what her hands had landed in.” Luke smiled in between laughs. “She scared my horse Duchess into a corner.”

“By the way, how did you find yourself in horse poop? I allowed you to be escorted by one of the most chivalrous men on the ranch.” Doc Fisher wiped the tears from his eyes from laughing so hard.

"I'm afraid she tripped and fell over my horse's hoof. I tried to get a hold of her arm, but she was out of reach." Luke smirked at Sophie.

Her cheeks get hot remembering the almost kiss. The chance of kissing a man had sent her into a panic. Sophie wasn't ready, and she didn't need Luke to get the wrong impression. "Well, some of us aren't blessed with as much grace as others. I've always been accident prone. It's been a memorable day."

"Well Sophie, get Callie if she'll come to you and let's head back to town. Hopefully, I won't pass out on the way. Wesley, if you see the buggy stranded on your way back to town, I hope you'll brave the smell and revive us." Doc Fisher grinned at him.

"I'll risk my own life to see you safely home." Wesley grinned.

Luke went up the steps while Doc Fisher helped Sophie and Callie get settled in the buggy. "Wesley, why don't we chat on the porch about your experience with cattle and how long you'll be staying in these parts?"

"Have a good afternoon gentlemen." Doc Fisher snapped the reins above the horse's backs.

Sophie had never seen Uncle Jared strike a horse with a whip but he used the noise it produced to get their attention. They trotted toward the tall posts which marked the way to the ranch. *Uncle Jared must be in a rush to get me home.* If it wasn't for the awful odor coming from her sleeves, she could've napped on the way back. Instead, she tried thinking of ways to get to her hotel room without her mother seeing her, or maybe she should say smelling her. Being the high-society woman she was, she'd be horrified her daughter landed in horse manure. Not the impression she'd prefer her to make.

Sophie tried to process all that had taken place. Had she wanted Luke to kiss her? Part of her had while the other part had jumped away. He must find her appealing. She'd always imagined herself married to a lawyer or another doctor, never a cowboy on a cattle ranch. Where had those images come from? She hadn't even decided if she liked him. He was handsome, but they didn't have much in common. Her head hurt. It must be from the fumes. She needed a warm bath to wash the stink and all these thoughts away.

Thinking of Luke would wait for another day.

Chapter Nine

Wesley went into the bunkhouse to get his bandana. It kept the sun off his face and the dust out of his mouth. He'd been at the Brown ranch for two weeks and had picked up the routine. He liked this job better than any other he'd had.

It worked well for him in many aspects. Miss Leland agreed to live in Nacogdoches to help the Browns with the home for orphans. She'd be moving to the Brown ranch in the next couple of days with his sister, Katie, and Patrick. Since Miss Leland decided to stay in Nacogdoches, she hadn't needed Miss Baker to keep Patrick. Megan Anderson had arrived too. Megan was the sister of, Ben, the ranch hand who'd been murdered taking Mrs. Brown into town a few years ago.

It was well-known around the ranch what had occurred surrounding the death of Megan's brother, and what had happened to Anna, now Mrs. Brown. This family had been through a lot. The gossip among the ranch hands was good regarding the Browns and how they treated everyone. Mr. Brown respected Luke as if he was his brother. Luke had already taught Wesley what would be expected of him. It wasn't anything he couldn't handle.

He typically rode out early in the morning with the other ranch hands to check on the cattle, make sure they were in good health, and repair any fences. The men had welcomed him and he enjoyed riding the range. It's all he'd done since he left New York.

While out riding the pastures yesterday, he'd discovered something odd and later spoke of it to Luke. A section of fence had been torn down. They did a head count of the cattle, and they were all accounted for. Luke asked him to keep an eye out for anything else he might notice that looked suspicious. It might've been a bear or other wild animal or it may have been cattle rustlers.

Wesley hoped the damage was from wild animals. He didn't wish to confront any cattle rustlers. They were as dirty and mean as they came. The outlaws understood if they got caught they'd hang, so shooting you was the best choice for them.

"Are you gonna stand there all day holding your bandana or get on your horse and accompany the men?" Luke laughed as he slapped him on the back.

"Sorry, I was daydreaming. I'm joining the men." Wesley tied the bandana around his neck. "I hope we don't have rustlers plotting to steal a big portion of Mr. Brown's cattle."

"Yeah, it troubled me when you described what you observed. Joshua may be riding out with y'all."

"I'm glad, it will be nice to get his take on the situation."

"There are black clouds on the horizon. We get tornados from time to time, the last one about three years ago. Hope it's just a rainstorm but keep your eye on it. If any funnel clouds form head back to the ranch.

We built storm cellars if we need them. We just completed the third one since the orphan home will be bringing more in. It's our biggest cellar yet. We can fit forty people in there if you squish them. The cellar near the barn will hold around twenty-five and the one near the house twenty. We might dig another one next year depending on how many children come here.

This ranch is expanding into quite the operation. I wonder what it's going to be like when lots of children are running around. We'll need to fence in an area for them to play." Luke grabbed two biscuits off the table as they walked toward the bunkhouse door. He threw one to Wesley.

Wesley took a bite of the biscuit. "I'm glad we're worried about the safety of everyone here. It's too bad we can't build a shelter for the animals."

"I agree, Wesley. Every time we've had tornados I dread to hear how the animals have fared." Luke opened the door and Wesley followed him out.

The sun peeked over the treetops to the east, casting a golden glow across the sky. He loved to look out over all the land. When he'd lived in New York City, he felt like a rabbit in a cage. The buildings blocked all views. He was glad to leave there other than missing Katie and his family who were gone. A sense of hopelessness and desperation gripped the city in chains. There were too many people and not enough jobs. Disease ran rampant because people lived so close to each other in squalor and starvation.

Joshua Brown met them at the doors to the barn. His horse saddled.

Wesley untied his horse's reins from the fence and

pulled himself up on his horse.

The men were ready.

Joshua mounted his horse. “Let’s search for clues to why our fences are being torn apart. Is everyone armed?”

Everyone nodded, and they took off toward the upper pastures.

As they came upon the fence, they noticed it was down again. This time the damaged area was wider.

Joshua examined the posts and wire. “It’s not an animal. The wire has been cut this time. Since you repaired the fence yesterday, they realize we’re on to them, so they didn’t even try to disguise it this time. There are hoof prints too. If we did a head count, I bet some will be missing. We have cattle rustlers helping themselves. Which means we’ll need men out here at night patrolling the pastures.

I’ll ride into town and let Sheriff Allen know. There should be four men in each pasture. We’ll rotate men so they don’t have to be out here every night. I’d hoped it wouldn’t be cattle rustlers. They must assume we’re easy pickings, but they don’t realize who they’re messing with. All of you realize the character of these cattle rustlers. They’d rather kill you than be captured. So if you run into them and they won’t surrender, shoot them. Some of you ride back and grab enough supplies for everybody tonight. We should have enough men so they only have to work a night watch every third day.”

Wesley volunteered for the first night. He counted on it gaining him some respect with the other ranch hands. They had to catch these rustlers. He’d witnessed their ruthlessness on the cattle drives. He didn’t want a gunfight, but that might be what it took to end this.

~

"How'd it go last night, Wes?" Luke slid off Duchess and led her into her stall.

"We never heard a leaf rustle. They must've been watching us and noticed we were on guard duty all night. I haven't asked the other men what they saw. Are they back yet?" Wesley got the saddle off his horse and laid it on a bale of hay in the stall next to Luke.

"Yeah, nothing happened there either. We need a better plan. They're not going to do anything with so many men watching. It protects our cattle but doesn't lead to us catching who's behind this." Luke handed Wesley a horse brush.

"They're gonna wait us out before they try rustling any more cattle." Wesley felt the fatigue of not having any rest with each stroke of the brush down the horse's side.

"They're not amateurs. When you get done, catch some sleep. The Browns are holding a big dinner tonight to celebrate the opening of the orphan's home and they want everyone there. There will be lots of good food and maybe some dancing. Although, finding a female dance partner might be difficult, as there aren't too many here." Luke went out of the stall. "See you this evening."

Wesley walked to the bunkhouse and laid down. He'd wash later because all he wanted now was sleep. His stomach rumbled, and he thought about eating but knew he couldn't stay awake.

He wondered who'd be at the party tonight. It might allow him a chance to speak with his sister. He needed to figure out the appropriate time to reveal he was her brother. Katie didn't recognize him when he'd met

Miss Leland and Doctor Knowles by the lake.

Hmmm, now there were a couple of beauties he could dance with. Miss Leland was living at the ranch as was, Megan. He doubted any of the three would be lacking for dance partners tonight. He hoped to dance with each of them.

Thoughts of holding a woman in his arms brought a smile to his face. He hadn't made time for women. Cattle drives were long and dirty and at the end of them, he'd leave for the next one. He'd saved a large amount of money to bring his sister back until he'd been out of work the last two years and had to live on it.

It was a blessing in disguise that his sister was put on an orphan train headed to Texas. Otherwise, it could've been years before he'd saved enough to get a small place and bring her out west from New York. She might have been married before he built a home. Wesley couldn't stay awake any longer as his eyes closed.

Chapter Ten

Luke put on his best shirt and tie. He contemplated what the evening would hold. Many of the Brown's friends were coming to celebrate the opening of the orphan home. They decided to name it, Anna's House, since it had been her dream.

Luke wandered over to where the tables were set up. He knew they'd be piled with food and he wasn't disappointed. Doctor Knowles and Doc Fisher were speaking with Joshua and Anna. He wondered what to make of Sophie's reaction to him trying to kiss her. He hadn't planned on kissing her. Although, when she turned and gazed into his eyes, he didn't resist. She jumped away quicker than he'd ever seen any animal move. He had to admit a part of him enjoyed her landing in the horse manure. She probably considered a cowboy beneath her even if he was a foreman.

Luke noticed Katie and Patrick pulling Miss Leland over to a swing. Ben's sister, Megan looked uneasy, so he went over to her.

"How are you this evening, Miss Anderson?"

"I'm fine. Please call me, Megan. I've never attended large parties. We kept to ourselves. Being busy is the best medicine for calming one's nerves. So, I'm bringing the desserts out."

"I've never been comfortable at this type of gathering either. I had a small family, and we lived ten miles away from the nearest town. Is it easier being here this time?" Luke put a cookie in his mouth. "Had to make certain they tasted good."

"You can be the taste tester." Megan laughed. "It is easier, I've had time to heal. I didn't want to leave before, but when mother became ill, I had to return. I can't believe she's gone. The only family I have left is a brother back east in North Carolina."

"I'm sorry Megan. Missing loved ones is painful but now you have a big family. That's how I see everyone here. Soon children will be following you everywhere. I learned two little boys are arriving next week. Their parents were caught in a flash flood and swept away. The boys are staying with a friend of the family. They don't have any relatives, so they are alone in the world." Luke eyed another cookie but didn't want to look like he had no self-control.

"It's not easy. I'm thankful for my faith. How sad for those little boys. I hadn't heard about them yet. I only knew we'd have Katie and Patrick. I'm glad Miss Leland agreed to stay. It would've been too much for one woman." Megan cut the pies into eight slices.

"Nice to talk to you, Megan. I should probably greet some other guests. I'm certain we'll speak again before the night is over." Luke turned to see Doctor Knowles alone near the drink table. He felt thirsty.

Luke snuck up behind her hoping for a reaction. "How are you, Doctor Knowles?"

Sophie jumped. "My, you do know how to startle a

lady. I'm fine. How are you Mr. Nelson, I mean Luke?"

Luke walked around her and grabbed a cup. "I'm having a great day, Doctor Knowles, I mean Sophie. I prefer to be unpredictable because if people are predictable they tend to be boring."

"I don't expect anyone would ever accuse you of boring." Sophie took a sip of her drink.

"I'll accept that as a compliment. Did your sleeves come clean from their unfortunate demise?"

Sophie's cheeks turned a bright shade of pink. "Yes, they did. All is as it was before. You might do a better job cleaning out the horse stalls though."

"They're cleaned every day. Usually, I don't have women falling into horse manure to get away from me." Luke gulped the last of his tea.

"I presume it's not the reaction you expected, but I hadn't thought you would try to steal a kiss either."

"Oh come now, Sophie, you turned your head and batted your beautiful eyelashes at me. What did you expect I would do?"

"I did no such thing."

"You most certainly did."

Sophie took a step away. "We shouldn't be having this conversation, someone might overhear."

"Would it ruin your reputation to be kissed by a mere cowboy?" Luke stepped closer to her.

"There you two are. At least there's no manure smell this time." Wesley grinned as he strode closer.

"We were just talking about that incident, although I get the notion Sophie would rather forget about it." Luke winked at her.

"I'm positive I'm not the first woman to feel that way." Sophie smiled at Wesley.

Wesley poured a cup of lemonade. “A truer word has never been told. I’m surprised you have dealt with it so well.”

Sophie crossed her arms. “Do you both think women are just fluff and incapable of dealing with difficult situations? You do understand that in order for me to cut someone open, fix what’s wrong and sew them back together, my constitution must be pretty tough.”

“I wasn’t suggesting that you weren’t, Doctor Knowles. May I call you Sophie, titles get in the way when you’re trying to communicate. I meant most women from the northeast would’ve been horrified having their hands covered in manure.” Wesley laughed.

“Please don’t confuse me with most women. Now you’re laughing at me again? I need to find Anna. She’s definitely an example of a strong woman. Have a good evening, gentlemen.” Sophie turned and sauntered away.

“Well, she told us.” Luke filled his cup again.

Wesley looked at Luke. “Yeah, that one won’t be easy to tame. She’s a high strung filly for sure.”

“An understatement. We’d be wise to pursue other women who’d welcome our intelligence.” Luke almost laughed at his own words.

“You may be right. I’ll say hello to Miss Leland. I haven’t spoken with her since I ran into her and Doctor Knowles at the lake a few weeks ago.” Wesley filled his cup. “This lemonade sure is good. Can’t wait to eat some of this food.”

“It won’t be long.” Luke scanned the crowd. He saw Sheriff Allen. “Excuse me, Wes, I’m gonna see if the sheriff heard any news about the cattle rustling." Luke decided to take a break from women. They were far too complicated for him.

~

The musicians tuned their instruments. A white circle in the darkening sky would soon turn into a bright light. The sun setting behind the hills turned the heavens into a painter's masterpiece.

Luke could hardly move after all the food he ate. Two helpings of chicken, potato salad, rolls, vegetables and two slices of apple pie. How would anyone dance after such a feast?

He wanted to go back to the bunkhouse and call it a night, but they expected him to stick around for a while. The proportion of women to men assured the women wouldn't lack for dance partners.

Luke planned to ask Megan and Miss Leland, but he was hesitant after being turned down by Sophie. Not too long ago, Luke had hoped to court the schoolteacher, Miss Baker. She, however, had her eye on Joshua, that was before Anna stole his heart. Luke lost interest in her after she'd cast him aside.

Luke worked long hours and seldom went to town which made it challenging to meet ladies. He wanted a wife and family, but to be honest, he doubted it would ever happen.

The musicians were playing a lively tune to get everyone moving. Although, only the children seemed interested in dancing. Miss Leland was nursing a cup of punch while Megan was picking up the food and taking it into the house. His first dance would be with Miss Leland if she agreed.

Luke started toward her, but one of the ranch hands

beat him and whisked her out onto the dance floor. The music slowed, and he noticed Joshua and Anna making their way out to dance. *She must be doing pretty good.* Luke turned to go back to his seat and bumped into Megan, knocking an empty bowl from her hands which shattered when it hit the ground.

"I'm sorry, I didn't realize you were behind me. Let me clean it up." Luke picked up the pieces of glass and threw them into a bucket.

Embarrassed, Megan headed back to the food tables to gather more empty dishes.

Luke followed her. "A break from cleaning is in order, would you honor me with a dance?"

Megan glanced at Anna, who happened to be dancing with Joshua a few feet away. Anna smiled and nodded her head.

"I would love to, Luke."

Two songs, two dances and they were ready for lemonade. Luke enjoyed having her as a dance partner. She followed his lead, and they floated effortlessly across the floor.

"I'm sure you're tired after working all day and now cleaning up." Luke poured her a cup of lemonade.

"I am exhausted. Although I enjoyed dancing with you, that's not work but fun." Megan took a long drink of her lemonade.

"Thank you, you're a great dance partner. Did you attend many dances in Louisiana?" Luke followed Megan to a table where they sat down.

"Not at all. My parents didn't have much money, so we never had pretty dresses. We got by with hand-me-downs. Not too many young men would invite a girl who wore raggedy clothes. It worked out all right as I had my younger siblings to take care of. My mother took in laundry and father fished on a boat long past dark."

"I find it hard to believe young men wouldn't ask you to a dance because of your clothing. You're a beautiful woman, Megan. Any man should feel privileged to have you with him." Megan glanced at her hands, her cheeks turning pink.

"I've never felt pretty, although Ben always told me I was. I miss him so much. Did you and Ben talk?"

"Yea, we talked in the evenings. Sometimes we worked together, but many days he'd be on one side of the ranch and I'd be on the other. He was a hard worker and a good friend to a lot of us. We're all like family around here. He'd figure out ways to make tasks easier. You should be proud. We all miss him too. Weaver was as mean and bad as they come. He didn't care who he hurt as long as he got what he wanted. If I could do that day differently, I'd send twenty men with Anna. I hold myself responsible."

"You can't take that guilt on, it's Weavers. Tensions were escalating between Anna and him over the mistreatment of the boys in his care. Then, after he brutalized and almost killed one of them, the law was after him too. Things were going to boil over at some point.

Ben and Anna were who he chose to take it out on. Ben wouldn't want you to blame yourself. There are evil people, they are the ones responsible for the wrong choices they make. We can only live the days we're given. I'm glad Ben lived them well." Tears appeared in Megan's eyes as she turned her head. "I better get the food in the house."

"Thanks for your healing words. They help. I've carried guilt with me ever since he got killed. Let's talk again." Luke stood up and walked with Megan back to the food tables. "Would you appreciate some help?"

"Thanks for the offer, but it's part of my job. It would be like me asking you to help build a fence. I would enjoy talking another time. Have a good night, Luke."

"You as well. I'm heading to the bunkhouse. It's an early day tomorrow. Well, every day starts early."

Luke walked to the bunkhouse whistlin,' *Dixie*. He'd enjoyed his time with Megan. Who needed highfalutin women who assumed they were too good for you. *Megan understands my life so much better.*

He couldn't imagine what would come of this. Hope breathed new life into him tonight. He should even sleep well. Anna's House might be valuable in ways he'd never imagined.

It gave children a home when they'd lost everyone. Because of Anna's House, the ranch had more women around. It should only get better from here.

Chapter Eleven

Sophie woke with a headache. Yesterday had been a terrible day. She had looked forward to attending the opening of Anna's House, but she hadn't expected Luke would try her patience so much. She'd always enjoyed being with people, but when she was around him she became someone she didn't recognize.

She sat by her uncle the entire evening while Miss Leland became the belle of the dance. Luke danced with Megan a couple of times. Even the schoolteacher, Miss Baker, was never without a dance partner.

A couple of ranch hands asked her to dance, but by that point, she was humiliated, rejected and didn't want to. Wesley occasionally glanced her way, but he never came over to visit. Instead, he ended up being one of many who danced with Miss Leland. He'd also danced with Katie which had tugged at Sophie's heart. How sweet of him to think of the young girl.

It was perhaps for the best, anyway. Why would she choose to share her life with a ranch hand? Although, in this town, it'd be hard to find a man of higher upbringing. The men were either older, had families or worked on one of the many ranches. Coming to Texas had been a mistake if she wanted a husband, so it's a good thing she didn't. She'd focus on being the best doctor she could, instead of who danced with her. Still, it miffed her only a couple of men had asked her to dance.

She missed her father and mother and wished they'd stayed. She loved Uncle Jared, but it wasn't the same. Life here varied greatly from the way she'd been brought up and life in general in Philadelphia. Men in Philadelphia were more empathetic to a woman's emotions. They wouldn't have made fun of her falling in horse manure or wanted to cause her any discomfort. Although, she wondered what these empathetic men said when the women weren't around.

People said what they thought in Texas, they didn't hide behind masks. The more she considered it, the more she realized she'd acted snooty yesterday. She'd never noticed herself being conceited, but in reality, she was every bit her mother's daughter. Sophie felt embarrassed for the way she acted. If she continued with that kind of attitude, no one would want to be around her.

Did she believe she was above Luke and the other ranch hands? She'd been born into a family who had wealth and a valued place in society, it had nothing to do with her. She had worked hard in school, but so did many students. Her family's social standing had opened doors for her. But, once the doors opened, she still had to prove she could do the work. *Wasn't that something to be proud of*? She paused in her thoughts and heard a voice in her head, "*Yes Sophie, but not an, I'm better than you kind of pride.*"

Callie whining interrupted her reflections. Sophie

needed to take her for a walk. Maybe she'd stop by the bakery. The smells which permeated the air from there was divine. She would pick up something for her uncle too. She'd work on being friendly, so when people wanted a doctor they'd know and trust her. Today, it's the bakery, Tomorrow… Who could guess?

~

Sophie knocked on the door of the Brown's ranch house. Anna had sent a note to her via a ranch hand asking if she'd visit her today. Her uncle told her to go as she needed to be around the women. So, she grabbed her puppy, her medical bag, and rode with Stephen out to the ranch.

Each day this past week she'd called on a different business offering her friendship and letting them meet the new doctor. Some business owners were welcoming, others rushed her out the door or pointed out that it wasn't right for women to be doctors. Mr. Garrett at the mercantile told her a ranch owner was bringing a male doctor in, so when her uncle retired they'd have a man they could count on.

Hearing this hurt Sophie. It wasn't a surprise to receive these sentiments, but it stung. Her teachers in college warned her women doctors were not accepted and considered being less educated than men doctors. Also, most guys weren't comfortable having a woman examine them. Sophie found this to be hypocritical since women had no choice in accepting a man to check them and deliver their children. At first, Sophie felt uncomfortable examining men when she was at the hospital, but it didn't take long before she understood as a doctor she needed to get over it.

"Sophie, dear, come on in." Joshua's mother opened

the front door.

"Hi Clara, you look wonderful, I'm here to see Anna."

"Oh, look! You brought Callie to play with her brothers and sisters. Here, I'll take her out back. Anna is feeding little James but I'm positive she'd be fine with you going in. Or, you can join the children and me in the kitchen for milk and cookies. I'll put Callie with her mother and siblings."

"I'll join you so Anna won't be rushed with her little one. She sent a note asking for me to come." Sophie followed Clara through the house and into the kitchen. Clara opened the back door. The puppies barked with excitement when she put Callie down to reunite with her family.

"Those puppies are so cute! Anna informed me she asked you to visit, but she didn't explain why." Clara poured another glass of milk. Sophie sat next to Ella.

Ella gave Sophie a hug. She asked how many patients Sophie had looked at in the last week. She talked about helping Luke a couple of nights ago when one of the mares gave birth.

Ella described how incredible it had been to see the foal being born. She asked Sophie if she might come to town one day and look at the doctor office. Doc Fisher always came out to the ranch if they needed him, so Ella had never been to his office.

Sophie told her to show up anytime. Seth and Rebecca described the games they were playing with Katie and Patrick. They were glad more children were on the ranch. Emily showed Sophie her new doll dresses Grandma Clara made.

The back door opened and Luke, Joshua, and

Wesley came in.

"Nice to see you, Doctor Knowles." Joshua ruffled Seth's hair. "I imagine these four have talked your ear off."

"They've been a delight. There's plenty to learn from each of them. I've loved every minute. It gets lonesome at the office when my uncle is away, so I enjoy their conversations. You're blessed to have such wonderful youngsters." Sophie smiled at the children.

"I agree. I'm glad they've shared some cookies with you." Joshua patted Clara's shoulder. "Are there any left for us, mother?"

"Of course son, I always bake plenty. Help yourself. We might even make room at the table for all of you." Clara scooted her chair over.

Wesley grabbed a chair and sat next to Sophie. "You decided not to brave the barn today?"

"I find the house much more to my liking. No unexpected surprises." Sophie glanced toward Luke who had sat on the other side of Ella.

"Well, no one would have discovered this country if they'd stayed in their homes. Along with risk can come great rewards. Studying to become a doctor and move to Texas shows you're far beyond remaining in your home." Luke put a cookie in his mouth.

"I agree. It takes a lot of determination for a woman to succeed in a profession mostly performed by men understanding most people won't accept you." Wesley grabbed another cookie. "You make the best cookies, Mrs. Brown. It's worth working on the ranch just to eat these."

Luke laughed. "Let's pay him in cookies."

Sophie didn't know what to say. Luke and Wesley

paid her a compliment. “I found out there’s a rancher in Nacogdoches bringing in a male doctor. He discovered I’m replacing my uncle when he retires, so he wants to establish a new doctor in town. I hoped people might be more accepting of a woman doctor in Texas, but I should’ve known better. If I can’t get enough patients to provide for myself, I may go back to Philadelphia.”

“Certainly not, we need you here. Anna and I will be seeing you.” Clara sat back in her chair. “Once all the women are aware you’re here, you’ll have many patients.”

“If their husbands let them. For some reason, too many people think the education a woman receives is less than a man’s, even though she does the same studies and exams. It’s hard to change what’s always been, but as time passes, there will be more and more women doctors.

God gave women a special gift to nurture and care for those who are hurting. It only seems natural we’d be good doctors. I’m not saying men aren’t good doctors, but I’m hoping to get that opportunity somewhere.” Sophie took a drink of her milk.

“I hope so too.” Ella smiled at Sophie. “I can’t wait to learn everything from you about becoming a doctor. If I don’t help people, I might doctor animals. You just got here, you have to stay for a while.”

“My uncle says to give it some time, so I will. In the meantime, you can ask all the questions you want, Ella. Although, working with animals is important too. You’d be very good at either.”

Anna walked into the kitchen with the baby. “Oh, you’re here Sophie. I’m glad you came. Let me snatch a couple of cookies and some milk, then we can sit and visit on the back porch. The temperature was nice when I was out a while ago hanging clothes out on the line. The weather is taking a turn toward summer."

Sophie picked up her glass of milk and half-eaten cookie and followed Anna out to the back porch. They sat in two white rockers in the shade of a big oak tree. The puppies were wrestling and running in the backyard. Vines with yellow flowers climbed along the posts on each corner of the porch. The water on the nearby lake shimmered like stardust with rolling hills of green grass and wildflowers behind it.

"You've made this place so homey, Anna. You step out here and immediately peace ebbs its way into your soul. Sitting here I'd forget all my cares in a matter of minutes. You built the bunkhouse, the barn, and Anna's House off to the side so they wouldn't obstruct the view. This will become a place of healing for many children who have been through horrendous things."

"Thank you, Sophie, that's my heart's desire. I understand what it's like to have nowhere and no one to go to. It doesn't take long to become a victim of someone looking for easy prey. I hope to make an impact by preventing that from happening with the children in our care. I wish I could do more, but we have to start somewhere."

Anna took Sophie's hand and looked her in the eye. "It's along these lines that I asked you here, Sophie. You believe you are called to follow in your uncle's footsteps as the town doctor, and perhaps you are. I've spoken to Joshua, and we'd love for you to live here and be an on-site doctor at Anna's House, our family, and the ranch. We have lots of accidents, big and small, sicknesses, and who knows what may come. You should see other patients, especially the women in this area, being there for births or other medical issues with their children.

However, we know it will be hard for most men to be comfortable seeing a woman doctor. I believe one day that will change, but not fast enough in Nacogdoches to keep you doing what you've longed for. When you're not busy, we'd love to employ you helping the children at Anna's House work through any emotional traumas as well. Someone with a good ear and heart and a love for God can help us understand and get through the bad stuff. You would let God lead you."

Anna continued. "It was painful for me to accept and understand what I'd been through, but once I did, my life changed profoundly. You've doubtless heard the rumor Mark Cole, who owns one of the biggest ranches around, is bringing in a male doctor.

To be honest with you Sophie, I see the wisdom in that. Some ranch hands and men who pass through our town can be less than honorable. They may take advantage of a woman who's alone in her doctor office, or take advantage of you on a house call. I came here thinking I could handle whatever happened, but found out I had no idea how evil some people are. I almost lost my life and one of our ranch hands was murdered by the evil I'm speaking about.

Right now, your uncle is going on all the house calls, but one day, he won't be able to. Please don't be offended Sophie because you are as good of a doctor as any man. I expect our ranch hands will go to you for most of their medical problems. They would see a male doctor for their personal issues, just as most women will choose to see you for theirs."

"Anna, I never expected anything like this when I got your note. Does Uncle Jared know?"

"We did speak to him first to make sure he wouldn't be upset if we offered this position to you. I'm certain he'll speak to you about it. What I can report is, he agreed to the idea. We asked him if he'd like to live at the ranch too once the doctor Mark Cole is bringing in gets here. With the two of you here, we might be capable of training younger women to be nurses or men and women to become doctors, at least get them started down the path toward it. Ella can talk of nothing else since she met you.

This is a lot to take in and I tend to jump ahead of myself, but I want you to understand the big picture. If you agree to do this but aren't happy then we'd let you leave, no obligations."

"You're a woman of vision Anna. Your ideas are fascinating. I thought I'd find a friendlier attitude toward women doctors in Texas, but I've discovered it's no different from Philadelphia. Where would I live if I moved to the ranch?"

"We're building a few small homes not far from the ranch house for Miss Anderson and another for Luke and for the future cattle foreman when Joshua decides who it will be. Miss Leland would've had one too, but we agreed she should live in the home we built onto the back of Anna's House. She can be close to the children and any problems that may occur.

We'd build yours above the ranch house on the other side. So people who needed a doctor wouldn't have to go through the ranch to see you. The other homes will be beyond Anna's House. But if you'd be more comfortable being back there, you could.

Your home would be bigger. We'd make the front part of your home an office where you'd examine your patients, comparable to your uncle's office. We'll let you design what functions the best for you. I can't express to you how exciting this is to me, Sophie. Once we started Anna's House, all these other ideas kept coming to mind. If you wanted a fenced yard and garden the men would do that too.

Maybe we'll have our own little town one day. We'd pay you a salary that we both agreed upon and you'd have use of our stables. There's plenty of beef and we want to raise more farm animals too, so everything we need will be right here. Joshua believes in this vision, and I hope you will too."

Sophie rocked back in her chair. How had this opportunity opened up for her? Might this have been God's purpose in bringing her here, not to take over her uncle's office? The possibilities were intriguing and exciting at the same time. She'd wire her parents and get their opinion. Sophie needed to pray about it too.

"Can I have a week or two to consider it? I'm humbled by your offer, Anna. You hardly know me, yet you see something in me you're willing to take a chance on. I'd never dreamed of such an opportunity. Working with mothers and children would be wonderful for me as I'd wanted to focus on that, but was told I would not find a job if I did." Sophie smiled. "I guess they were wrong."

"In their world but not in ours. This makes perfect sense for us, having a doctor on the ranch because we'll have lots of children here. In an emergency, by the time someone rides into town to get the doctor and rides back, it might be three or four hours. With some injuries that would be too long. I want the children who come here to recognize we value them and their health. It also demonstrates how much we love and care about them. God has blessed us with a prosperous ranch and this is how we choose to make a difference with what we've been given."

"This is an extraordinary vision, Anna. There's nothing more precious than children."

"Let's go in. We've discussed most everything. I'd love for you to live and work here Sophie. Isn't it amazing how unpredictable life can be with all its twists and turns? Although, nothing takes God by surprise. He's preparing us for each new step.

I'm anticipating what we're accomplishing here will be an example of how to make things better for orphaned children. Hopefully one day more people will have the same desire and strive to make it take place. If we all do something it makes a big difference. Did I say I'm happy you're here?" Anna hugged Sophie as they went back inside.

Chapter Twelve

Fence posts lay broken in the muck. The rustlers cut more fence and drove cows through without anyone noticing. The cattle thieves hadn't been back for a few weeks, Wesley had hoped they'd left. Now twenty head of cattle were missing and Wesley knew why.

Life had taken an upward swing for him but this might send it crashing back down. He'd been grateful to accept this job and see his sister again. Now, there were outlaws taking the cattle he was expected to keep safe.

He'd head back to the ranch and speak with Mr. Brown. He needed to know what Joshua wanted to try next. Wesley wondered if other ranches had cattle missing. He walked the damaged fence line searching for clues as to who these men were. He discovered nothing. Wesley mounted his horse and headed back. He wondered if Mr. Brown would regret asking him to be the cattle foreman if he didn't catch the cattle rustlers. He needed this job in order to provide a home for Katie and himself.

Men, women, and children were going about their day when Wesley rode up to the barn. It was a busy place. Anna's House now had six children they were caring for. Doctor Knowles had accepted Anna's offer to be the ranch doctor, so a few men were hard at work building her office and house. Miss Leland and Miss Anderson worked all day at Anna's House. Mrs. Brown, Anna, had brought in another woman and her son as well.

Luke confided to Wesley his responsibilities were more than he'd been able to keep up with since the building began. He helped build so his time taking care of the animals had been cut in half. He spent his evenings making sure the other men had done what they should've.

When Luke had a free moment, Wesley noticed it was always spent talking with Miss Anderson. The other ranch hands said he'd been close to her brother Ben before he was murdered. Wesley wondered what went on between Luke and Doctor Knowles because they avoided each other like the plague.

Although, that didn't bother Wesley because he found her fascinating and wanted to get to know her. He wondered if she had any interest in him. She kept her feelings locked up. Sophie was a doctor who'd always had the best, her father an important lawyer. He was an orphaned drifter who did what it took to survive.

His goal had always been to provide a home for his sister. He hadn't let himself become involved with anyone, but he hadn't stopped thinking about Sophie. Her long golden brown hair, hazel eyes, and charming smile captured his attention from the moment he first encountered her by the lake. Hiding his feelings was becoming harder and harder. She'd been spending a lot of time at the ranch deciding how she needed everything in her new office to be.

Thinking of Sophie must have brought her to the ranch because he recognized her buggy as he rode closer. He jumped off his horse and walked inside. Mr. Brown was at his desk in the entryway.

"Wesley, what brings you back so early today? Joshua stood. I'm guessing it's not good news."

"I wish it was, but more cattle have been rustled. I counted twenty head missing. I discovered a section of fence destroyed where they passed through. I assumed you'd want to look at it."

"I can't go up there today. I'm about to leave because I'm meeting with other ranch owners about what's going on. Have you scheduled a group of men to stay there tonight?"

"Yes, I moved them around a bit so we'd protect different areas." Wesley removed his hat. "Do you want me to head back?"

"You've got men assigned, so they can do without you for the night. I need a favor. I would've done it myself but I have to leave."

"What do you want me to do?"

"Doctor Knowles came here with Doc but he had to leave. He took one of our wagons. Shortly after, a ranch hand from the Carson ranch stopped by and said their boys were sick. They wanted Doc to check them as they didn't need the new baby catching anything. Doctor Knowles said she'd go but Doc doesn't want her going alone. Can you be her escort? You arrived just in time. I can't take anybody away from what they're working on here, they're all busy."

"I can do that." A few hours alone with Sophie in a buggy. Wesley wondered how he'd gotten so lucky.

"Good. Get a fresh horse hitched to their buggy. I'll ask her to be ready by the time you're done."

Wesley led his horse to the barn trying to contain his happiness. He had dreamed of being alone with her, and now it was happening.

~

"I'm glad the Carson boys will be all right and it wasn't serious." Wesley tried to help Sophie into the buggy, but she insisted on getting in herself. She hadn't talked much on the way to their farm. He supposed it'd be the same back to the ranch. His chances of making an impression were dwindling.

"Yes, it's a stomach malady and they should be fine in a few days. Nothing to worry over, but it's good they made sure. They're such a nice couple. I understand why the Brown's like them."

"Yeah, they were nice. It's getting late, I hope we make it back to the ranch before dark. You may need to stay at the Brown's tonight unless your uncle is waiting.

They were about half-way when the wind picked up and Wesley wondered if they should've remained at the Carson's ranch. Dark clouds rolled toward them making the day darker by the minute. Wesley didn't want to frighten Sophie, but the clouds were dense and he worried they'd form a funnel. Finding shelter for a thunderstorm was much easier than a tornado. That was a whole different scenario.

Wesley scanned the area for a rock formation or cave where they might wait out the storm. He'd hadn't been this way until today. He remembered the stories ranch hands told of past tornadoes. He'd never witnessed one and frankly, hoped he never would. In the distance, he noticed a cleft in a rock formation and believed it'd be big enough for them to get inside.

"Doctor Knowles, or can I call you Sophie? I asked before but you never answered. I don't want to upset you, but we should find shelter. These clouds are growing dark and moving in such a way that I'm concerned about a possible tornado. I hope it's only a thunderstorm, but I don't like taking chances."

"Oh, my! If it's for the best, I agree, I don't wish to take any chances either. I've never experienced a tornado, but they can be devastating. Yes, call me Sophie." She shuddered.

They made it to the rock cleft, and it was bigger than Wesley had expected. They should be able to get the horse inside with them. Wesley hoped he'd have enough time to gather wood and build a fire.

"Sophie, did you bring any supplies we might use?" Wesley unhitched the horse.

"Clara gave me blankets, hard tack, biscuits and a canteen of water. I set them behind the seat. She said you can never guess what the weather will do, so be prepared. I haven't eaten hard tack before. Clara told me it takes getting used to."

Wesley looked behind the seat, "Remind me to thank her when we get back. I brought my gun and an ax. I'm going to find some firewood. Can you take those supplies inside the cave?"

"Of course."

Wesley chopped and gathered enough wood for the night. He led the horse inside and tied it to a boulder. The wind grew in strength and noise and a loud howling sound intensified. Wesley was glad they found shelter. The rain drizzled at first but soon developed into a full-fledged monsoon. He built a fire, then stood next to the log where Sophie sat. She was quiet.

"You doin' alright?" Wesley added another branch to the flames as he sat beside Sophie.

Sophie glanced at him. "I'm a little concerned but have been praying. God can get us through this."

"I expect He understands you better than He does me."

Sophie drew her shawl tighter around her. "He hears all of us when we pray. I'm sorry you don't feel like He does."

"Do you need one of those blankets yet?" Wesley looked behind him where they lay.

"I'm all right for now."

"When I lost my parents, I asked Him for someone to help us and no one did. So, I headed out west hoping I'd find a steady job that would support me. It's been inconsistent until Mr. Brown hired me. This is the first job I've been able to count on."

"So He did provide. Maybe not in the way you wanted, or when you wanted, but in His timing. You wouldn't be here if he'd answered your prayer sooner."

Luke considered that for a moment. She was right. He provided a good job when he needed it most, right when he located his sister.

Sophie looked in the bag by her side and pulled out a canteen, the biscuits, and hard tack. "You first."

"I've had it before. Not something I would ask for, but it's edible."

Sophie took a bite and gagged. "I'm not sure about the edible part."

"It actually grows on you the hungrier you get."

"If you say so. I'll stick with the biscuits." Sophie took a drink of water from the canteen then gave it to

Wesley.

"Thanks."

A burst of lightning lit up the darkened sky accompanied by thunder which vibrated the earth under his feet. A deafening roar with a huge flash of lightning made them both jump. "Wow, that was close. It's going to be a long night, hopefully, we can sleep." Wesley gave the canteen back.

Sophie looked up. "What brought you to Nacogdoches?"

Wesley got distracted looking into her eyes. "I'm sorry, what did you say?"

"I was asking how you ended up in Nacogdoches."

Wesley didn't want to discuss anything about his sister yet. He was waiting for the right moment to reveal who he was. He wasn't ready to share much of his life.

"Just going from town to town seeking decent work, and the next thing I realize, I'm in Nacogdoches. Seems like a nice place, and I've got a stable job. So I suppose I'll be sticking around for a time. Why would you give up the comforts of home in Philadelphia to show up here? I listened to your story. You wanted to see if people would accept a woman doctor out west, but I bet your father would've set you up somewhere and championed your abilities enough to encourage people to give you a chance."

"You might be right, but I chose to do this on my own merit. I preferred to become the doctor I've always wanted to be without my father's help." Sophie took off her hat which allowed her long brown curls to tumble down her back.

Wesley was smitten. He had to put his hands on the

log so he wouldn't touch those curls. "That proves what type of woman you are. Most people would've taken the easy way."

"I don't know about that, but I'm glad I didn't. I miss my parents, but I can't wait until my house and office are finished. I'll be able to practice medicine the way I was trained. My uncle is a great doctor, but so many things have changed since he learned medical procedures. He's adopted some newer techniques but is still stuck in some of his old ideas. Mr. Brown and Anna are supporting me in using new medical instruments and tools which will help care for people better. How long do you plan on remaining with the Browns?"

"I'm not sure. I assumed I'd work a month or so and be on my way. Now I'm going to be the cattle foreman and am considering staying for as long as they'll have me. I prefer getting a stable wage and being around everyone on the ranch. It's like being part of a family again. I've learned so many new things. Someday I want to have my own place, but this is a good fit for now."

"Yes, the Browns are so welcoming and try to encourage everyone they cross paths with. It's rare you encounter a couple so generous and eager to serve those around them."

A loud clap of thunder made Sophie jump and Wesley placed his arm behind her to keep her from falling off the log. She immediately moved forward away from his touch. He rose and strode to the opening of the cleft. Rain streamed down, changing small trenches into streams. He hadn't witnessed it raining this hard since he'd been in Texas. It was dark now, and he hoped they had enough wood to make it through the night. He walked back to the fire.

"If we lay down as close to the fire as possible we should be somewhat warm. I'll keep the fire going through the night, but it won't be blazing because we'll run out of wood. It looks like we have three blankets but if it becomes too cold, we might have to sleep back to back to stay warm."

Sophie gasped. "I couldn't do such a thing."

"You will if you get cold enough. Gossiping will happen at the ranch anyway with the two of us being alone for the night."

"I still can't. Let them gossip, at least God and I will know nothing happened."

"Don't be upset. It shouldn't get that cold since it's raining and its early spring. Your honor will be safe with me."

Tears fell down Sophie's cheeks. She wiped them away and turned her head.

"Why are you crying?" Wesley sat next to her again.

"I don't know. I'm scared and upset. I've never been alone with a man and you're right, people will gossip, they always do. I'm already looked down on as a woman doctor, who knows what else they'll say now. I've never gotten myself into compromising situations.

"They might, they might not. I shouldn't have mentioned anything. We'll be fine. It's a bad storm, but we're safe in here. There aren't any tornados forming. I realize you don't know me well, but I wouldn't take advantage of any woman. My mother and father taught me to cherish women and help them.

I'm certain everyone will understand we had to seek

shelter because this is a bad storm." Wesley wiped a tear from Sophie's cheek as he stared into her eyes. He trailed his hand down her face and she shivered. Tears still slid from their shimmering depths. His body moved closer to her, and he leaned his head within inches of hers. He watched the flickering emotions in her eyes.

He'd only kissed one woman in his twenty-five years, but never one who would change his life. This was a defining moment. If he took this step, Wesley would be committed to letting his heart love, and she might break it. Sophie stayed close. She closed her eyes, and he didn't refuse the invitation. He brushed her lips lightly with his. Still, she remained next to him. He caressed her hair, the silky strands were everything he imagined they'd be. He kissed her this time, not expecting, but cherishing. She placed her hand on his chest. He wanted to draw her closer and kiss her with all the passion inside of him, but he wouldn't upset her. He pulled away but remained close. He played with the strands of her hair and she moved closer. She wasn't making this easy. Tenderly he kissed her then dropped his hand.

Wesley looked into her alluring eyes. "Moving away isn't what I wish to do. You don't understand how beautiful you are and how you're making me feel. I'd never want you to be afraid. We should put those blankets down and get some sleep. We can head back at first light if the rain stops."

"I've never kissed a man."

"Well, this man hopes you'll save all your kisses for him

In the firelight, Sophie's face turned red. He traced her lips with his finger. "It's all right, it's a normal thing between a man and a woman who are attracted to each other. We haven't done anything wrong." He tilted her face toward him. "You might expect me to know a lot about this but I don't. I've only kissed one other woman, and it was on a dare from some men I was around. I resolved I wouldn't kiss someone until she mattered to me.

I've been thinking of you since we first met at the lake. I didn't want to scare you away, so I've waited to see if you were attracted to me." Wesley pulled her close and she laid her head on his chest.

"I'm sure you haven't had an issue with women being interested in you. All I hear in town is how handsome the new man at the Brown's ranch is and wouldn't it be marvelous if he would come a courtin.' They talk about how green your eyes are and when you look at them everything else fades away."

"They may feel that way but how do you feel, Sophie?"

"You've already figured it out. I let you kiss me when I've never let another. You have your arms around me and I'm not moving away. I wouldn't even mind if you'd kiss me again." Sophie stared into his eyes and this time he kissed her how he'd wanted to before.

"Sophie, we should stop before things go any further. We don't want the gossip to be true. I'll add some more wood to the fire while you lay out the blankets."

She put the blankets on top of each other. Maybe she'd gotten over not wanting to be next to him. This was going to be a long night if he had to ignore her laying against him. Then, she placed a blanket down the middle. *I spoke too soon.*

When they laid down she turned away from him.

"Good night, Wesley."

"Night, Sophie."

"Thank you for being a gentleman."

"I'm trying."

Sophie giggled.

He loved the sound. "You should laugh more often, Miss Doctor. It suits you."

"I'll try."

Before long she'd fallen asleep. He sat up for a time and watched her. Her long eyelashes resting on her cheeks. Other men spoke about how their wives looked like angels when they slept. Sophie wasn't his wife, yet, but she looked every bit like an angel. Where had that thought come from? How would Sophie fit into his plans?

Wesley laid down and recalled the evening. He'd be eternally indebted to whoever created this awful storm. Wesley had never experienced anything like this with a woman before. He wanted her to be a part of his life, but making that take place wouldn't be easy, he held no delusions on that. He rolled over on his side as he observed each breath she drew in the firelight. It wasn't long, and he fell asleep.

Chapter Thirteen

Sophie opened her eyes and panic seized her. Someone's arm laid over her. Then, she remembered they had sought shelter in a cave, and the arm over her was Wesley's. She relaxed. Every breath Wesley exhaled on the back of her neck sent shivers down her spine. So much for putting a blanket in between them, it didn't keep them apart.

She listened for the rain but only the quietness of early morning greeted her. Someone from the ranch might be searching for them. It wouldn't be appropriate to find them together. They'd have a hard time persuading them of their innocence. She longed to always feel this safe and cherished her whole life.

This man had surprised her with his tenderness. His kisses were chaste, except for the last one and she'd asked for it. Still, he'd not pressured her for more. Guilt wiggled its way into her consciousness. Did she behave how she should've?

The emotions he stirred in her opened her to the possibilities of what marriage would be. Only two men had tried to kiss her, Luke almost accomplished it but she'd leaped into the horse manure. When Wesley touched her cheek to wipe her tears she didn't want to move away, only closer. She found it hard to believe the man every woman in town gushed about cared for her. His long dark hair and beard accentuated his strong face, and she wanted to caress his cheek.

Her lips still felt the pricks from his beard where he kissed her. She needed to think on other matters and spend time with God once she got home.

Wesley moved and drew her closer. "Good morning beautiful." He whispered in her ear. "We found a way to be next to each other."

Sophie melted into his words.

"I can't imagine a better way to wake up." Wesley ran his fingers through her hair.

Okay, she needed to get up. Now!

Wesley kissed her neck and her legs turned to mush. Her mind reeled from the urgency to get up. But the kisses trailing down her neck held her in place. She'd just lay here a minute more.

A branch snapped outside their cave. Wesley bolted up and grabbed his gun. "Take the blankets and go over by the horse," he whispered.

Sophie picked up the blankets and drug them behind her to the horse. She folded them as Wesley walked toward the opening of the cave.

"Wesley! Is Doctor Knowles with you? We've been worried since you didn't come back last night. We hoped you'd stayed at the Carson's ranch. We rode there first thing this morning, but they said you both left before the storm hit. We didn't notice the buggy on the road as its well concealed behind the bushes."

Wesley walked out of the cave. The voice belonged to Luke. Wesley bought her some time. She finished folding the blankets and tidied up her appearance. She had no idea how she looked. Her hair probably stood out in a million different directions. She smoothed down her skirt and blouse and wrapped her shawl back around her. Sophie heard the men talking.

"Yes, she's here. When I noticed how dark the clouds had become and the wind began howling, I realized we needed to find shelter. I hoped there wouldn't be tornados, but we couldn't take a chance. We found our way to this cave as it's all I saw. I chopped wood for a fire to keep us warm. I'm glad I made that decision. I can't imagine traveling in that storm."

She appreciated this man even more. He cared how they found her. She took hairpins out of her medical bag. She always carried a few pins in there and struggled to smooth and pin up her messy hair. She hoped it looked half-way normal.

"Quick thinking, Wesley. A few small tornados touched down, one not far from the ranch. We didn't have any damage other than some fallen branches. You did all the right things. Doc will be relieved to have her home unharmed. Let's hitch the horse to the buggy and get you both to the ranch. I'm sure you're hungry."

"You might say that. We had water, hard tack, and a couple of biscuits Clara gave her. I ate a few bites of the hard tack but Soph... Miss Knowles gagged at the taste. I'll bring the horse so we can get him hitched."

The man was good. It made her wonder if the innocence he'd espoused last night had been completely true.

Wesley touched her hand. "Are you ready to face them?"

"I guess. But, I'm anxious."

"Don't be. Be the innocent angel you are. If they read shame or guilt, they'll feed on it like sharks. Men talk and Luke's impression will be told to Mr. and Mrs. Brown." Wesley grabbed the reins and led the horse out.

Sophie followed a few feet behind him carrying the blankets. She didn't feel so innocent.

"How are you doing Doctor Knowles?" Luke asked as she stepped out of the cave.

Sophie kept her head bent. "Other than being tired and hungry, I'm fine and thankful we stayed safe. Although, it got scary at times with the wind, thunder, and lightning." She stuck the blankets behind the buggy seat.

"Like I said to Wesley, we saw a couple of small tornados touch down not far from the ranch, so it's a good thing you guys found shelter. Your uncle is worried, so we best go home. We brought an extra horse, Wesley, in case your horse ran off scared from the storm."

Sophie got in the buggy as the men finished hitching the horse. They set out with Luke and a couple of ranch hands in the lead and Wesley behind them on the extra horse. He turned and winked at Sophie. She smiled back.

She was grateful Luke didn't ask countless questions, but she knew her uncle would be interrogating. He'd want every detail, but many moments she wouldn't be sharing. Those secrets would forever be locked in her heart.

Sophie observed the man invading her thoughts as he rode in front of her. She'd let Wesley kiss her and more than once. She fell into the horse manure evading Luke's kisses. When another man had tried at a dance Sophie walked into another room. The emotions inside of her for Wesley took her by surprise. Every single woman around was attracted to his looks, but her affections ran deeper as if they'd always known each other.

Wesley had been an orphan, a drifter and now a ranch hand. Sophie, a doctor brought up in one of the wealthiest families in Philadelphia. Yet, nobody ever attempted to learn who Sophie was on the inside, as Wesley had last night. He wore loneliness like a cloak and apathy a shield from brokenness. She sensed his life had been much harder than the little he'd told her. He wanted to succeed and create a life to be proud of.

Sophie recognized his desire to accomplish goals as she wanted the same. She grew up in a family without siblings and parents who always had a dinner or party to go to. Sophie knew loneliness, it wrapped its arms around her every evening growing up. The servants her only companions in the big dark house at night. She loved her parents, but they'd never taken the time to be with or understand her.

The cure for her loneliness came when a friend asked her to go to church one Sunday when she turned fifteen. She'd agreed, and that day changed her. Jesus made life bearable and gave her purpose. He never left her.

Her heart grew heavy and Sophie realized she rushed into this. Wesley might be a good man, but it didn't mean he was the right man for her. Her mind had always been her driving force in life, but last night she'd let her heart rule. Sophie hoped her affections for

Wesley weren't misplaced.

The ranch came into view as they moved across the countryside. Her reasons for choosing to live there grew stronger now, she wished they'd finish her home soon. Sophie needed her mother or someone she might talk openly with. Anna would be who she'd go to if Wesley didn't work for them. She couldn't create any problems for him. He told her last night how much he appreciated his job.

Luke slowed his horse enough to be next to her buggy. "Did everything go all right last night? He didn't try to take advantage of you, did he?"

Sophie tried not to let her embarrassment show but the blush on her cheeks might betray her. She hoped he'd assume it emanated from her not wishing to reveal such matters.

"It went well, and no he didn't. He sought to calm my fears and assure me we'd be all right. Just as I assume you would've done."

"Of course. I'm glad he didn't take advantage of the situation. Some guys would've. We don't need those type of men working here. I want to talk to you soon when you have time. We got off on the wrong foot and I'd like to clear things up. I'm not quite the cad you consider me to be."

"I don't think that of you, and I'm sorry you assumed I did. You caught me off guard and I overreacted. If you wish to talk, then that would be fine. Maybe once I am moved out to the ranch?" Sophie didn't look at Luke but she kept her eyes straight ahead.

"I'll let everybody know nothing happened between you and Wesley. You needed shelter because of the storm, and when we found you it looked innocent."

"Thank you, Luke. I worried about it last night and this morning. I never considered what might take place when you require a man to accompany you and no one else is around. I realize more and more every day that Anna and Joshua giving me this chance to do medicine on the ranch is a real blessing."

"They're great at helping us out even when we don't recognize it. Joshua is my best friend and Anna has been a blessing to everyone. I'm glad you had someone with you. Well, we're home and I'll let you reunite with your uncle alone. Have a safe trip to town."

"Thank you again, Luke."

Luke rode up to the lead and Wesley fell back beside her.

"What did he want?"

"He wanted to make certain you'd acted like a gentleman. After answering his question, he said he'd tell everyone nothing transpired between us and we didn't have a choice other than to seek shelter." Sophie glanced at Wesley. "He was nice about it all."

"I'm glad he believed you. Although, I expect he may be a little sweet on you, so not sure I want him hanging around you much."

"You said he liked Miss Anderson?"

"He could, but if he had a chance with you that might end it. There's not a woman around prettier than you."

Sophie smiled. She peered toward the ranch house and saw her uncle and the Brown's sitting out on the front porch. "Looks like we have a welcoming committee."

"Guess, we better get ready for the interrogation." Wesley rode up by Luke and the other men as they stopped in front of the ranch house.

Chapter Fourteen

Luke walked a line of fence with Joshua and Wesley. It had been two weeks since Wesley discovered the twenty head of cattle missing, and sometime over those past two weeks, they'd stolen thirty more. The ranch couldn't sustain itself with loses like this as fifty head of cattle would be an enormous amount of money.

Sheriff Allen told Joshua a couple of other ranches had a few head stolen, but they were hitting the Brown's ranch the hardest. The cow hands tracked them a few times, but the trail always led to nowhere as the cattle rustlers covered their tracks well. The Brown's ranch covered hundreds of square miles. The over one thousand head of cattle he owned were so dispersed across his land he couldn't possibly guard them all while having any men left to work at the ranch.

Wesley scanned the rolling hills outside the ranch land desiring to see movement. "The rustlers must be continually watching us, then going to where we ain't."

"We need to do something different. Instead of waiting for them to come to us, we take the fight to them." Joshua gulped water from his canteen. "Let's send out men in groups of three or four who are continually on patrol outside of the ranch borders. We'll confront any strangers we discover along the path. We place the men about a mile apart so if any gunshots are heard, the closest groups are within distance to help. We'll get some men from other ranches willing to help since our ranch is getting hit the hardest."

"That sounds like a better plan, Joshua. What we're doing now ain't working. We need to switch it up. Luke pulled himself up on Duchess.

"Let's go home and work out the details, then I'll contact the other ranchers and see how much support we can get. Joshua put the canteen back in his saddlebag and got on his horse.

Luke followed behind Wesley and Joshua, deep in thought. They'd never dealt with organized cattle rustlers before, only a few small time thieves. The penalty for cattle rustling is hanging, so you had to be really good or really stupid to risk it. This time, they were really good. It bothered him they continued to come back for more. They must not think the men from the ranch posed much of a threat to stop them.

Why now? What had changed to make them vulnerable? They'd lost Jim who'd been a great cattle foreman. A tough man, who knew every square mile of the ranch and commanded respect. He'd shocked everyone when he unexpectedly quit and left them without another foreman. Wesley was young and understood a lot about cattle but he didn't have experience being a foreman of men older than him. Luke wasn't sure if he could handle the job.

Wesley dealt well with the storm emergency with Miss Knowles, by making a quick decision that saved their lives. However, Luke had the impression there may have been more to the story than either of them owned up to. He'd noticed Wesley almost called Miss Knowles by her first name after they found them. Miss Knowles had officially moved to the ranch two days ago, and he'd noticed she and Wesley ended up in the same place at the same time quite often. Luke promised Miss Knowles he'd inform everyone they had no choice but to hunker down for the night in the cave because of the storm and nothing happened between them. But Luke had doubts, which rankled his pride.

He'd been attracted to Sophie, but she'd preferred horse manure to his kiss. If that didn't injure a man's pride enough, preferring Wesley over him certainly succeeded.

Luke had been flirting with Ben's sister, Megan, since the celebration at the opening of Anna's House. He couldn't tell what she thought of him, but she acted glad to see him. Her dimples and beautiful smile radiated the kindness in her heart. He missed his good friend Ben. The way his life ended had been tragic. He enjoyed reminiscing with Megan about Ben as she revealed details of Ben's childhood he hadn't known.

Luke hadn't had many opportunities to speak with women. He stayed distant so he wouldn't get hurt. When he took a chance, it generally ended as it did with Sophie, any interest died, before it had a chance to develop.

Dust swirled in the wind as they galloped through the gate to the ranch. Children played in front of the house. Doc Fisher must be inside since his buggy sat out front. He planned on moving to the ranch as soon as the new doctor, Mark Cole, set up his practice in town.

The Brown's had suggested building him a home near Sophie's. The ring of hammers pounding nails echoed everywhere. The men were busy doing chores. Luke took pride in how well the ranch operated, everyone worked together to accomplish what needed to be done.

He wanted his own home. He'd thought about buying his own ranch or asking Joshua if he'd sell him a chunk of land. He'd like some land off one of the pastures to raise horses. With the amount of people working and living increasing at the ranch, he envisioned this place becoming a town one day. Now that they had an orphanage and a doctor, a school should be next. They'd need a restaurant or big building to feed all the people who worked here. It'd be nice to have a boarding house for relatives and visiting family. A mercantile or two would be great additions so they didn't have to go into town for the loads of supplies they required on a daily basis. They'd only need a post office and a church after that. Having a pastor would be a support to the orphans and of course to everybody else as well. If a church was built, he might even be persuaded to attend.

They dismounted next to the barn. Luke needed to get Duchess watered and fed and hoped Megan might be outside. Maybe she'd offer him a cup of lemonade. He'd envisioned Wesley and Miss Leland together, but that died as quick as it started. Wesley only had eyes for Sophie.

Luke brushed Duchess. She loved this time of day, occasionally it looked like she smiled at him. Since he'd taken over as the foreman at the ranch, his duties prevented him from riding as often as he used to. He felt every mile they rode today. A swim in the lake might revive him, but he imagined the water was pretty cold. Did Megan like to fish? He should ask her sometime if she'd like to go. He knew where the best fishin' holes were. She'd surely have a good time cause they'd be assured to catch lots of fish.

As he walked toward the bunkhouse, he noticed the sun sinking below the hills. It wouldn't be long until dusk settled over the ranch. The day's work activities would end, dinner devoured, then a few men brought out their mouth harps, guitars and played and sang while others played cards. Life was simple, but not easy. They worked hard and earned the time to unwind. He savored every minute of every evening.

Well… almost. Lately, he'd spent many nights guarding cattle from the thieves that roamed in the night, and tonight would be no different. The evil men needed to be rounded up and shot or hung for what they'd done.

These outlaws preyed on the younger cattle and calves because they were easier to steal. But the calves had a strong instinct for returning to their mother even when separated by miles. To keep them from running back to their mothers, these evil cattle rustlers did cruel and brutal things to them. They cut the muscles supporting the calf's eyelids, to make them temporarily blind, or applied a hot iron between their toes to make the calf's feet too sore to walk, or even split the calves tongue to prevent suckling.

Luke had no tolerance for these heinous cowards who had no mercy in their hearts for men or animals. They needed to be stopped one way or another, and if that meant shot or hung for their crimes, so be it. If this ranch became a town one day, he'd become the sheriff.

He'd always wanted to be a lawman.

~

Luke partnered with Wesley and one other man. This was his fourth time guarding the pastures. The men rotated so every other day they spent the night on watch. Every night, six to eight groups of three men walked the fences, depending on if they had guys helping from other ranches. Since thirty head of cattle disappeared a few weeks ago, the rustlers hadn't been back. The new plan of going after them instead of waiting for them to strike seemed to be working. This monotony had to end, the outlaws needed to be arrested.

They'd been patrolling the bushes on foot since ten and Luke imagined the time to be close to three or four in the morning. He couldn't wait for the next couple of hours to pass by so he could head back to the bunkhouse and his bed. They tried to be as quiet as possible so none of them spoke, it had been difficult to keep moving when all he wanted to do was sleep. The other groups of men spread out around the pastures. They hadn't heard any noises or seen any movement.

A sliver of moon barely lit the dark and cold night. A slight breeze rustled the surrounding leaves. Even with multiple layers of clothing, the cold crept in and chilled him to the bone. He didn't know how the other men felt but he needed to make those rustlers pay for every hour he'd been out here.

Wesley got Luke's attention and pointed to a place in the pasture where the fence disappeared into a grove of trees. Shadows moved. Luke saw shapes of men creeping along the fence line. How many were unknown, but it looked like quite a few. They had to inform the other men without creating noise. Luke whispered to the ranch hand next to him to quietly gather the other groups. They'd need the support because they were outnumbered.

They could've used the expert marksmanship of Joshua tonight. They waited for what seemed an eternity, watching the shadows cutting wire and digging out posts with speed and efficiency. Had Luke and Wesley not been observing them they'd never have realized they were close. Twelve of their men showed up. Luke sent one to inform everyone at the ranch and then go to town for the sheriff.

"How many more do we have out here?" Luke whispered.

"We only have another nine men out tonight, but they're quite a distance away. It will take some time for them to make their way here." Wesley leaned over so Luke could hear him.

"We'll wait a few more minutes and then make our way over there but spread out so we surround them. I doubt they'll surrender, so when we get close we'll remain behind cover and shoot to kill if they refuse to surrender. Let everyone know." Luke took a deep breath. Every muscle in his body felt as if it would pop at the slightest movement.

If he was a praying man, now would be the time to say one. Luke whispered to Wesley. "Pray much?"

"Not really," Wesley responded

"Well, that's more than I have, so you might say one for all of us. I don't like how this looks, we need more men who can shoot. How is your shooting skills?"

"I like to think I'm pretty good."

"I hope so," Luke said as he kept his eyes on the

rustlers.

Three more men showed up, they had fourteen now. Some rustlers had moved the cattle toward the opening. They couldn't wait much longer to act. He certainly never wished to be in this position again so they had to end it tonight. Their objective wouldn't be easy.

"Don't let anybody get away and don't get shot. Let's start moving into position. We can't wait any longer. Keep low and spread out. When we get there, be loaded, and ready to shoot." Luke got on his haunches and crept toward the rustlers as he ducked behind the bushes. Wesley and everyone else followed behind him. "Get ready, I'm going to shout at them to drop their weapons and surrender."

"Take cover and get ready to fire," Wesley whispered to the men.

"Drop your weapons! We have you surrounded!" Luke shouted.

Gunfire erupted at the sound of his words. Luke and his men fired back. A couple of men wailed, they'd been hit. The gun battle raged as the sound of bullets whistling through the bushes filled the once quiet night. Not one rustler had fallen. Luke hoped help came soon. He motioned Wesley to take some men and circle around behind the rustlers while Luke advanced toward them with the rest.

The gunfire slowed for a few seconds. Maybe the rustlers thought they'd killed most of them. Luke saw shadows in front of him moving in all directions. His men fired again, dropping two of the outlaws, yet the return fire increased. He didn't know how long they could hold their ground. Gunfire broke out from behind the rustlers, and another one collapsed, as Wesley and his men had made their way around to their rear flank. Just as it looked like they may be gaining the upper hand, a barrage of gunfire rang out from behind Luke, pinning them down without a chance.

One of the rustlers hollered, “Hands up and drop your weapons or you’ll be dead! What’s left of your posse is surrounded.”

“We’re dropping ’em,” Luke yelled with one arm up and the other throwing his gun to the ground. *This isn’t good.*

“Keep your arms in the air and drop to your knees.”

Luke and his few remaining men followed their orders. One by one the rustlers tied their hands behind their backs.

“Hey boss, look who we found. Our long lost buddy, Wesley. Guess, he survived that gunshot to the chest and somehow ended up here with these cattle ranchers. Wonder if they realize they hired an outlaw?” One of the rustlers pushed Wesley in front of everyone with a rifle in his back.

The rustlers tied up everyone except Wesley. One of the outlaws walked over to Wesley and slapped him in the face, bloodying his lips.

“So you managed to survive, huh? If you had better gunfightin’ skills you wouldn’t of got shot when we robbed that train. Good thing you got fixed up by that pretty little woman doctor or you wouldn’t of made it. You slowed us down, too much work to carry you around so we had to dump ya... Bet they don’t know you’re a train robber.”

Wesley stood his ground. “I should’ve guessed it was you lowlife gang of fools. You don’t care who you hurt.”

"At least I don't make no pretenses who I am, unlike you. One day a robber, the next a ranch hand. Trying to get a clean start, I suppose, huh, Wes? Guess, we spoiled it for ya. Did you find that little sister of yours, or just make up that sob story."

"I rode with you on the train robbery to ensure she'd be all right. I had no intention of taking anyone's money."

"Guess you didn't protect her too good since you took a bullet. Oh yea, the choir boy story. The orphan son trying to get his sister back. Seven years later and you still ain't got the money to take care of her. You should've come back to us and you would've had her by now. As it is now, you've guaranteed your death, cause you know who we are, and we ain't gonna be part of no hanging."

"Would ya prefer we shoot ya here or around back in private?"

Luke spoke up. "Let him go, take the cattle you have and leave. You have my word no one will follow you."

"This scalawag means that much to you, does he? Well, I ain't taking the chance." The gang leader spat on Luke.

Luke jumped to his feet and lunged toward the gang leader. A gunshot rang out and Luke crumpled to the ground. Pain shot through his leg and he groaned in agony.

"Count yourself lucky I didn't shoot ya in the head. Grab the chatty guy and Wesley and let's get outta here. These two might bring us a decent ransom."

Chapter Fifteen

The morning sun peaked over the horizon as Sophie sat down to breakfast with the Browns. They'd invited her to discuss how many days a week she'd be able to devote to Anna's House.

The front door flung open and slammed shut as a cowhand ran into the dining room.

"Mr. Brown, Mr. Brown, they've cornered the rustlers at the upper pasture. Luke sent me to get help because they're outnumbered. I gotta' find the sheriff."

"I'll get more men and some wagons hitched after I grab my things." Joshua leaped to his feet and headed up the stairs

"Oh, my!" Anna followed Joshua to help him get ready.

A knot formed in Sophie's stomach, causing her to gasp for air. Wesley went with Luke. She must keep calm and pray, otherwise, Anna and Clara would figure out her feelings for Wesley. Did it matter if they guessed? Maybe she needed to let them know. But now was not the time to do so. Sophie wasn't confident she could hide the fear gnawing at her heart.

Sophie excused herself. "I need to walk and pray. I

want to seek God's protection for everyone."

"Of course dear, do what you feel God's leading you to do. Come back when you're ready." Clara took more biscuits to the children.

Sophie walked past the lake. Luke and Megan had been fishing there only a couple of days ago. They were having lots of fun. She was glad Luke found someone who enjoyed his company.

Now that she'd moved to the ranch, she spoke to Wesley every day. She couldn't bear the thought of him getting hurt, much less killed. *Why am I wasting time walking when I should be preparing for serious injuries such as stab or gunshot wounds? Someone should tell my uncle.* Sophie ran quickly back. She saw Hank sitting outside of the bunkhouse.

"Hank, please hurry into town and inform my uncle we might have quite a few injured men brought to the ranch."

"Absolutely Miss Knowles. I've been sitting here wondering what I should do to help. Too old to ride after some cattle rustlers but I can ride to town."

"Thank you, Hank. Please hurry!"

Sophie ran back to the ranch house and into the dining room where Anna and Clara were sitting.

"You both must think I'm not a good doctor. I should be getting the medical office ready for any injured men. I sent Hank into town to get my uncle. Would the two of you mind boiling extra water, and if you have any cotton, you could tear into bandages, it would help tremendously. Do you think Megan and Ella might assist me? I haven't seen either of them. I promise I'll keep Ella away from any bad stuff."

"Ella went to help Miss Leland with the children

this morning. I'll get them over there. We'll boil water and make bandages." Anna stood. "Will you watch the children, Clara?"

"Yes. I'll pray and take care of things here."

"Thank you, both." Sophie ran to her medical office. She didn't have a lot of room, so if there were many injuries they'd have to move them to the bunkhouse. Sophie cleaned and sterilized everything. She prayed while she worked and imagined Clara and Anna doing the same.

~

The rumbling noise of horses and wagons coming into the ranch alerted Sophie that Joshua and the men were back.

Joshua burst through Sophie's office door.

"We have injured men. Do you want to check them to see which ones need help first? Has anyone gone for Doc Fisher?" Joshua held the door as she rushed outside.

They were lying the injured men on the ground. "Can someone get me more water and blankets?" She assessed each man's injuries to determine who she needed to work on first. Wesley and Luke weren't with everyone.

She asked Joshua where they were and if they were safe. He said the men told him the cattle rustlers took them. Sheriff Allen and his deputies were on their way, and they'd be riding back out to look for Luke and Wesley. He'd explain more after she attended to the injured men.

Sophie's heart sunk. Why would they take Luke and Wesley? It didn't look good. She had so many questions but had to focus on helping these men.

Sophie pointed. “Can someone bring him in?” She needed strength far greater than her own.

Chapter Sixteen

Wesley sat in the undergrowth, tied to a tree. The rustlers had blindfolded him and Luke, then taken them some place, miles away from the ranch. They'd removed the blindfolds a while ago. He wondered if help had made it to the injured men yet. Surely Joshua and the Sheriff were looking for them.

He had to get them out of here before Luke got worse. Luke's bullet wound was oozing blood as he laid next to him, hands still tied behind his back.

He looked pale and his breathing labored at times. They didn't care if Luke died, and they wouldn't let Wesley live either. It would be close to impossible to get Luke and himself away from this gang of thirty men. It couldn't hurt to pray, the odds weren't good, and they needed a miracle.

Clay, the gang leader, sneered as he walked toward them. Wesley despised the man. He'd dumped him in an alley of some town after the train robbery and luckily the sheriff found him before he died. Wesley made up the story that he was robbed to explain the gunshot wound. Riding with Clay's gang had been the biggest mistake of his life.

"Looks like he ain't doing too well." Clay kicked the bottom of Luke's boot. "Guess he should've kept his mouth shut. What are the odds we'd be rustling cattle from a ranch you were workin' for? I wonder how much the owner will pay for y'alls return. You'll be dead, but he won't know until it's too late."

"He's not dumb. Joshua will realize you don't intend on keeping us alive. Hard to say if he'll pay anything. Although, you might want to do something with his wound if you plan on using him to get money. They could ask to see us before they hand any money over." Wesley appealed to Clay's greedy side.

"I'll have one of the men put a bandage on it, but we're not diggn' no bullet out."

Wesley noticed another man headed toward them. He knelt by Luke.

"Why did you shoot Luke?"

"You know him," Wesley asked.

"Worked with him. One of the few men I admire."

"Who are you?" His face was covered with a bandana.

"I used to have your job and would've done a whole lot better too. These men offered me a chance at more money than I'd make for Joshua in ten years. I couldn't pass it up."

"If you live to spend it, you'll be lucky. Nice way to repay a man who trusted you and got your friend shot in the process. Mr. Brown is better off you left." Wesley spat in the dirt.

"We'll see. I'm leaving Clay. Meet you in our agreed upon place." The man walked toward the horses.

"You and your gang, ain't gonna be able to stay around these parts. You'll be hunted by every lawman and rancher in this area." Wesley wanted to get Clay talkin'.

"After we grab the money for you two, we're leaving for Mexico, buy some land and maybe a woman or two. Staying ahead of those Texas Rangers is too much work. If things get boring in a few years, I might come back and do more rustling. It's better than train robbery. Cattle don't shoot at you."

"No, but angry ranchers do."

"They try, but they can't out shoot us. You witnessed that, should've come back to our gang, Wesley. If ya had, you wouldn't be tied to that tree." Clay laughed.

"I couldn't live with myself if I had. My parents taught me to work diligently for a day's pay. You don't steal from hard working people."

"Life is to enjoy, I have no time for working. I got more than enough money to do what I want and haven't worked a day yet. Anyone who gets in my way won't be living long."

Wesley decided this banter wasn't worth his time. You can't argue with a crazy man. Clay didn't know the value in anything beyond himself, other people's lives meant nothing to him. The heartbreak he brought to the relatives of people he killed never crossed his mind. He was pure evil.

One of the grungy looking outlaws hollered to Clay. "Hey boss, we got word a train's passing through Nacogdoches and it's carrying lots of money. It'll be coming by later this morning. Should we rob it?"

"Did anyone get the ransom note to the ranch?"

"Butch nailed it to their front gate. He waited out of sight. A ranch hand retrieved the note and took it into the ranch house."

"We gave them till noon, right?"

"Yep, they have till noon to leave the money in a bag at the giant rock formation on the north end of their land."

Clay gathered his band of outlaws together and laid out their plan to hit the train. "All of us, except you two, are goin' rob the train. You two go out to the rock formation, with the bodies of them do-gooders strapped to a horse, get the ransom money and dump their bodies there. Don't come back here, just high tail it to Austin, and we'll meet you. Don't even think about not showin' up with that money or you can guarantee I'll hunt you down and put a bullet between your eyes. The law will be comin' for us, so we'll ride nonstop for the border."

After hearing their plans, Wesley knew their time was short. He had to try something soon. Although, their plan had given him an inkling of optimism. If all but a couple of the outlaws left to rob the train, he might be able to overpower the remaining two, if given a chance.

Wesley leaned his head back against the tree. He asked for God's help and that he'd get the chance to hold Sophie again. His thoughts revisited his memory of the night they spent in the cave. He wanted to spend a lifetime with her and didn't want their story to end this way.

His eyes kept closing. Wesley's mind wandered to his sister Katie and he hoped he'd get the chance to tell her he was her brother. He shouldn't have waited.

Luke moaned, Wesley wanted to help. He owed the man. He'd given Wesley another chance at life and he needed to find a way to take advantage of it. He wondered if God saw them. Wesley sure hoped so.

Chapter Seventeen

Sophie walked out her back door. Her uncle wanted to stitch up the last patient and told her to get some fresh air. They'd worked most of the morning without a break. The sun pushed toward midday. She added another prayer for Wesley and Luke. She must've said well over a hundred since they got the news early today.

They'd removed bullets from five men. Two were not doing well. One of them hadn't made it. The rest should recover. She couldn't think about the one they lost. When she became a doctor, Sophie told herself she'd need to be strong to cope with tragedy. Saying it and experiencing it were entirely two different things. She didn't want anyone else to die, so she had to be at her best.

Anna came by a couple of hours ago and said a ransom not for Luke and Wesley had been nailed to their gate posts. Joshua and the sheriff were figuring out the best way to handle it since they'd returned. Anna hoped her words brought comfort knowing the rustlers planned on keeping them alive to get the ransom money. She hugged Sophie and told her they continued to pray.

Sophie struggled to stretch every muscle in her body they hurt from being bent over working on the men the last three or so hours. They transferred each man to the bunkhouse after she or her uncle finished with them. Uncle Jared and she would alternate checking on them throughout the day. Megan, Clara, and Miss Leland stayed with the men to make sure they had what they needed. If they noticed any changes, they'd let them know. Ella stayed with the children.

Tears fell from Sophie's eyes as she worried over Wesley and imagined what he might be going through. She wished they'd spent more time together since their night in the storm. She'd been busy moving into her house and setting up the office.

Sophie looked forward to his smiles each day and the few minutes they'd find time to talk. They tried to keep their relationship a secret, but since Joshua told her the news about Wesley and Luke this morning, she'd realized they shouldn't have cared what people assumed.

Sophie loved Wesley. She couldn't bear the prospect of him not coming back. Didn't she believe in a God who performed miracles? Doubt and fear crept in. Her mind imagined every awful scenario taking place as her thoughts dwelt on it. The only way she might control the worry would be to keep busy and pray. She went inside.

Chapter Eighteen

Wesley had dozed off, but hearing horses running woke him up. They must be heading out to rob the train. He wondered who had stayed behind. He shouldn't have nodded off. He needed every minute to come up with a plan.

He looked at Luke's chest, hoping to see it rise and fall. It did. Luke hadn't woken up since he'd passed out on their way to the outlaw's camp last night.

He spotted one of the outlaws left to guard and kill them. He didn't recognize the man. He must be new. Wesley didn't want that ugly face to be the last person he looked at. He wondered where the rustlers had put his guns. He searched around him but they were gone. He always carried a small revolver in his boot. It felt like it was still there, they must not have checked. Would the guy let him up to do his business? He had to make sure there were only two.

"Hey," Wesley yelled. "My stomachs really botherin' me and I need to go if ya know what I mean. You won't want to be hauling my dead body smelling like I'd be smelling if you don't let me go, would ya?

"Hey Jack, did boss say he could get up?"

"He never said, Bill. If you keep a gun aimed at him, it shouldn't be a problem. There's two of us and he's unarmed, so you can let him go over there. In about an hour or so we'll be strapping him to a horse, and he won't be wanting to do anything except breathe. Jack and Bill starting laughing.

Wesley couldn't wait to erase the grin off Jack's face.

Bill came over, untied him from the tree and yanked Wesley to his feet.

Wesley's legs wobbled.

"Aren't you gonna untie my hands? How you think I'm gonna clean myself?"

Jack picked up his rifle and aimed it at Wesley. "Go ahead Bill, I got him in my sights."

"Turn and hold your arms out away from your body," Bill said. He untied the ropes that tightly bound his wrists.

"You'll have to give me a couple of minutes, I have no feeling in my arms," Wesley said.

"You ain't got long. Start walking over that way until I say stop."

This man must not be too smart, and Wesley was thankful for it. He walked about fifty feet, just inside the woods, when Bill told him to stop.

"Just letting you know, it might take me a bit."

"Don't go any farther!"

Wesley stopped and slowly turned, facing Bill with his gun pointed right at him. He pulled his pants down and squatted to do his business. His pants partially covered the front of his boots so Bill couldn't see his right hand digging for the pistol down the backside of his boot. He had five shots for two men and one was pointing a rifle at him, so he better make the first shot count. He felt his pistol and wrapped his fingers around the grip. He noticed the other man, Jack, wasn't watching him as he was cooking something over the fire. He'd need to distract Bill for a split second to set his plan in motion.

"Hey, Jack! Your boot's on fire! Wesley screamed and pointed with his non-shooting hand.

Bill turned his head for a second to look at Jack, and Wesley drew the pistol from his boot and got a shot off, hitting Bill in the arm, causing him to drop his rifle. Wesley quickly fired another shot at Bill and hit him square in the chest, knocking him dead off his feet. Wesley immediately turned toward Jack who moved toward his gun. He pulled the trigger and hit him in his hip, causing him to fall.

Wesley pulled his pants up and ran over to Jack as he laid on the ground moaning. "I guess it's you who won't be needing to do anything but breathe! I'll send the sheriff for you." Wesley hogtied his arms and legs behind his back. He picked up the guns and ran to Luke, who had opened his eyes.

"Luke we need to get outta here and I can't do it without your help. Can you hear me?"

Luke moaned.

"Come on Luke! We need to leave!" Wesley poured some water from one of the outlaw's canteens over Luke's face.

Luke stirred. He tried to sit up but groaned in pain.

Wesley got him to drink water. "Luke, can you make it back on horseback? I don't know this area like you do, so you need to get us home."

"I'm feeling a bit dizzy, but think I can make it."

Luke sounded better now.

"I've got to get you on a horse."

Wesley lifted Luke off the ground over his shoulder and managed to get him side saddle on one the outlaw's horses. He mounted the other outlaw's horse and maneuvered it around to the opposite side of Luke's horse so that he could lay back over both horses. "This is gonna hurt like crazy but we've got to get your bad leg over the horse." Wesley leaned over onto Luke's horse and drug him back far enough to reach his badly injured leg and pull it over the horse. Luke screamed in pain.

"Ok Luke. Can you ride alone or should we ride together?"

Luke was breathing heavily, still writhing from the pain. "I can manage. I'll let you know if I can't. We can go faster that way." Luke held on to the reins with a grimace on his face.

Wesley smacked Luke's horse to get it moving and followed right beside. "Do you have any idea where we are?" Wesley asked.

"I think so. Once we get past these trees, we can let them run as long as I can stay on. Running the horses will be a smoother ride and less jarring on my leg."

Luke would have a hard time staying on the horse, so he rode right next to him on the side of his bad leg.

They rode for what seemed like an eternity before he recognized the landscape. Wesley was a tough man, but he had tears in his eyes when the ranch came into view.

As they entered the ranch gate, Joshua and some of the men came running from the house and followed them until they stopped in front of Sophie's door.

Wesley jumped off his horse as Sophie came out the door running toward him, then into his arms. “I’m so thankful you’re back and not injured”

Wesley and Joshua pulled Luke down off his horse and took him into the medical office. “I’m glad I got the prettier doctor.” Luke tried to laugh through the pain

Wesley remembered his prayer and thanked God that he was able to hold the woman he loved again.

Sheriff Allen arrived and said he needed to question Wesley about what took place while Sophie was working on Luke and followed them inside.

Chapter Nineteen

Luke sat in the rocking chair on Joshua and Anna's porch with Megan beside him. She'd been his constant nurse and companion through his recovery. His leg had mended for the most part. He'd always walk with a limp, but at least he could walk and for that he was thankful.

He'd be forever indebted to Wesley for getting him out alive. When Luke heard the whole story, he realized what a remarkable man Wesley was and how lucky they were to have him. Luke was in shock when Wesley told him about Jim, their former cattle foreman. He wondered how Jim fooled them all while he worked on the ranch. Joshua and Luke had trusted him completely.

Wesley had been cleared of any charges pertaining to the train robbery and finally told his sister who he was. She'd been scared at first, but Katie, Wesley, and Sophie were fast becoming inseparable. Hearts were healing. They were a part of the ranch now and a much bigger family. All the years they'd been alone were being restored.

Megan spoke to him about God. His life had real

meaning for the first time. Luke asked Megan to marry him and planned on building a house for them soon. Joshua gave him fifty acres, he refused to sell it to him. He'd lend him the men to help build it too. How had he been so lucky to find Joshua?

On the day Wesley and Luke returned from being kidnapped, Sheriff Allen questioned Wesley. He told the sheriff the outlaws plan to rob the train and ride to Austin before moving onto Mexico. Joshua and Sheriff Allen rounded up seventy-five men and took off after them. They caught up to them in Austin because they were waiting for the two gang members they'd left to kill Wesley and Luke and get the ransom money.

There was a fierce gun battle that included the local Sheriff and his men as well. They killed Clay, the gang leader, and thirteen of his outlaws before the rest surrendered. They were arrested and put on trial and hung. They never found Jim.

A rightful ending for all they'd done, but a sad day for everyone who had been hurt. No justice could ever atone for the loss of loved ones. Choosing to murder and steal brought dire consequences and Luke wondered if they'd felt it was worth it in the end.

"Hey, Luke, how you doing today?" Doc Fisher walked up the porch steps.

"My leg's getting better each day. Glad I had such a good doctor taking care of me."

"She's becoming a great doctor. Her understanding of new ways to do things saved your leg. I would've amputated it. We're lucky to have her here, wouldn't you say? Doc sat across from them in a chair.

Megan put her hand on Luke's shoulder. "We're glad you're both here, Doc. We can't imagine how this would've turned out if the two of you hadn't been working together. Many more men could've lost their lives. I hear you've both been dealing with the stomach sickness going around. Did either of you get any sleep?"

"I've slept more than Sophie. She insists I rest. It's been a trial but we're on the mend now. You know Luke, you might even be able to dance a couple of slow dances with this pretty lady at the barn dance this Saturday. My suggestion for continued healing."

"I'll take you up on that as long as she's agreeable. I won't be doing any quick steps though that's for sure." Luke winked at Megan.

"You won't be able to get me away from your side, Luke Nelson." Megan kissed his cheek.

"That's music to my ears. I'll be dancing with the prettiest gal there." Luke leaned his head against the rocker. He tired easier than he used to, but Sophie assured him it was normal. His body would recuperate in time and he'd be back to his old self.

"Looks like someone needs a nap." Megan helped Luke out of the rocking chair. "I'll walk you to the bunkhouse. Then I will go to the orphanage."

"She's right. How can I argue with her anyway, Doc?"

"I wouldn't try."

Luke held Megan's hand as they walked past the barn. It was a warm day. Summer had arrived. Flowers were blooming by the lake. Maybe they'd go fishing this week. Luke had appreciated the time off while he got better, but he wanted to get on Duchess and race across those pastures again. Making Megan his wife would be the happiest day of his life. He'd come to understand how precious life was, and to cherish every moment with the ones you love, because, tomorrow is not a guarantee.

Chapter Twenty

The barn glowed from the many candles and lanterns placed throughout. Women wore their finest dresses and the men their best suits. The atmosphere hummed with excitement. Sophie mingled with other women while Wesley observed her from afar.

Sophie Knowles was a force to be reckoned with and went after what she wanted in life. Inside her heart of gold, he had somehow found a place. He didn't feel worthy, but he wouldn't change it for anything.

Sophie looked so beautiful tonight. Her hair pulled up at the sides into a pearl-studded barrette, curls cascaded down the back to her bare shoulders. The elegant green dress she wore brought an extra sparkle to her large hazel eyes. He'd let every man there knew she belonged to him.

A neighboring ranch offered to host a dance in honor of Sophie and her uncle. Word had gotten around of their heroic efforts to save the lives of many of the men wounded in the gunfight with the outlaw gang. Temperatures cooled as the sun fell from its afternoon perch. Celebrations gave everyone a break from the doldrums of life.

Sophie considered having an extravagant dance party excessive because doctors took an oath to heal the sick. Sophie insisted she wouldn't go, but as this evening got closer, she changed her mind. Wesley told her she should let the town folk show their appreciation because after all, they were embracing her as a woman doctor.

He looked forward to a night of dancing and holding her in his arms… and he would enjoy every moment.

They'd been learning a lot about each other. It took him time to explain his life and all that had happened to Sophie, but she wanted to take in every word. They realized she had been the one who saved Wesley's life after the train robbery. Although he'd been unconscious, he remembered hearing a woman praying over him. He thanked God a bandana covered his face that day otherwise they wouldn't be together.

Sophie understood his bad choices were based in love. He'd rode with the gang to protect his sister. However, she told him she didn't understand why he'd hidden his identity from Katie. Wesley believed he'd failed his sister because it had been seven years, yet she still had no home. He didn't want to face the disappointment in Katie's eyes, but Sophie expected he'd receive her love, forgiveness, and happiness. Turns out, she'd been right, because when Katie found out, she hugged him and cried. Two hearts had healed with one embrace.

Joshua offered to build Wesley a house, and he accepted. Wesley dreamed of a ranch of his own, but that would come later.

The band started playing and Wesley noticed

Sophie dancing with her uncle. He'd been daydreaming far too long. The rest of the night she belonged to him.

When the song ended, Wesley asked her for the next dance. As she took Wesley's hand, Sophie suggested her uncle ask Miss Clara to dance.

The band played a new waltz, and Wesley drew her close. "You're so beautiful Sophie. If I could only read your thoughts." Wesley whispered in her ear.

Sophie put her hand in Wesley's as they began to dance. "When Uncle Jared is around, Miss Clara acts younger and checks to see if her hair is in place. She must be attracted to him. My uncle has never married, and he needs companionship."

Wesley had hoped her thoughts lingered on him, but holding her close made the struggles of life disappear.

After dancing through four songs, he suggested they get some punch and cake and go outside. The brightness of the full moon outshined the myriad of stars. He led her to a bench, and they sat down. A small fire burned near the other side of the barn where men stood talking

They ate their cake and Wesley took hold of her hand. He'd longed for her kiss since the night in the cave.

"We need you two inside." Joshua waved them toward the back of the barn.

Wesley wondered why as they followed Joshua inside. As they entered the barn, everyone started clapping. Doc Fisher and Sheriff Allen stood on the stage with the band.

"Come up here you two. We want to honor you for all you've done." Sheriff Allen announced.

Wesley had no idea he would be included. The

cheers got louder as they walked on stage.

"The last few weeks have been incredibly hard for a lot of folks and thanks to these two doctors we've made it through. Many of you expressed your unhappiness when a woman doctor showed up to take our beloved Doc Fisher's place, but she has proven herself to be every bit as capable. Both she and her uncle, Doc Fisher, have saved life and limb as well as treated sicknesses with an attitude of humility, and I think I speak for everyone when I say thank you, Doctor Knowles and Doc Fisher!"

Sheriff Allen put his hand on Wesley's shoulder. "This man here, Mr. Wesley Johnson, defied all odds and miraculously saved Luke Wilson and himself from certain death by the guns of two cattle rustlers. Then he led us to them by revealing the information he'd gathered in their captivity. We're thankful for heroes like the three of you!" Everyone cheered.

"Wesley, you're probably unaware there's a reward for the apprehension of the outlaw gang. They'd robbed many trains, rustled cattle and murdered whoever got in their way. I have it here with me, and would like to present it to you." Sheriff Allen handed him a bag of money. "From all of us, thanks again, Wesley Johnson!" The audience erupted with applause and whistles.

The reward for their capture surprised Wesley. Maybe he'd buy some land with the money. It proved doing the right thing is always the best thing.

The crowd engulfed them as they walked off the stage to shake their hands and personally thank them. Because so many ranchers wanted to hear his story, he and Sophie were eventually separated by them. He'd make sure to plan some alone time with her tomorrow.

Chapter Twenty-One

Heat waves shimmered in the hot Texas sun. Sophie stepped outside and swept the dirt from her front porch. She'd been cleaning all day. Wesley and the men were working the cattle. She hoped he'd be back soon. It was a nice day… if you liked heat and humidity. Even with the windows and doors opened it still felt like an oven inside.

The dance held to celebrate them last night was nice, but she hadn't wanted the attention. She didn't need a party thrown in her honor to say thank you. She was just as shocked as Wesley when the Sheriff presented the reward. She wondered what he'd do with it.

Sophie brewed a cup of tea and walked toward the ranch house porch. Anna and Miss Clara were already there.

"How are you today, Sophie?" Anna sat on the porch swing rocking little James to sleep.

"I'm doing well, other than this heat is stifling."

Clara sipped her ice water. "It is hot in Texas. Takes a while to get used to."

The women spoke about what took place at the barn

dance and how happy they were for Wesley. The orphanage was doing well, and they were helping Megan and Luke plan their wedding.

The men returned from their work and led their horses to the barn, but Wesley wasn't with them. Joshua had been working inside and came out to join them. They talked a while longer until Sophie excused herself to prepare supper.

"You're welcome to eat here." Clara offered.

"Thank you, but I'll just make myself a sandwich. I'm not very hungry."

Sophie said goodbye and walked to her house. She opened her back door.

"Woof. Woof."

Sophie heard Callie's paws hitting the floor in the living area. She grabbed a broom in case an intruder might be inside. She peeked through the door and saw Wesley in the middle of the room holding a bouquet of wildflowers. She dropped the broom and hurried to his side.

The room glowed with the light from many candles.

"This room looks incredible."

"I've been waiting for you all day to leave the house so I might surprise you." Wesley handed her the flowers and a wrapped present.

Sophie smiled as she opened the gift. Inside the box, a gold heart on a chain shimmered in the candlelight. She held it up. A small diamond hung in the middle.

"The necklace is beautiful, Wesley."

"But you're more beautiful. Can I help you put it on?"

"Yes, thank you." She gave him the necklace.

Wesley swept the hair from her shoulders. His fingers brushed her skin as he fastened the chain around her neck. Goose bumps sent shivers down her back.

"I've fallen in love with you, Sophie Knowles. You stole my heart that night in the cave, and each day you fill my thoughts."

"I love you too, Wesley."

"I have another gift for you, depending on your answer to this question. Wesley got on one knee and reached for her hands. Will you honor me by becoming my wife?" He opened a small velvet box to reveal a diamond ring.

"Oh Wesley, I can't imagine anything else I'd rather do."

Wesley gently held her left hand in his, then slid the ring onto her finger. Sophie admired the ring. It had a large diamond set in the center, with two smaller diamonds on each side.

"Wesley, I love it."

He stood and took her other hand in his, their fingers intertwined. His lips touched hers gently.

Sophie had been longing for his kiss. She put her arms around his neck. Their kiss deepened. She didn't want it to end. Wesley leaned his head back and looked into her eyes.

"I can't wait to spend my evenings kissing my wife."

Heat rushed into her cheeks.

"Where will we live? What are your plans, Wesley?"

"Until we get our house built, we'll live in your home. I told Joshua I'd keep working for him. The reward is a nice sum of money. I asked Joshua if I could purchase some land and he agreed. He said he'd sell it to me for half its value. With the rest of the reward, we should be able to build a house, buy a couple of horses and a few head of cattle, so I can raise my own herd.

We won't be far away from your office. Just like your uncle, I'd prefer you not make house calls unless someone goes with you. Doc lives right behind you, so he should move into your home and let the new teacher at the orphanage live in his. I'm sure she'd appreciate having Doc Fisher nearby.

I love you Sophie and want to be a good husband. We should have lots of children and raise them in church. I believe God answered my prayer when Luke and I were being held captive by the rustlers. He gave me a way out when there was no way. I considered our escape to be a miracle. I'd like Katie to move in with us if you agree."

Sophie reached for his hand. "Of course Katie will live with us. When we have children, I won't make house calls. The new doctor in town can handle those. I'm sure tending to the needs of the ranch and orphanage will keep me busy.

I love you too and can't wait to be your wife. You found a way into my heart and broke through my mistrust."

Wesley wrapped her in his arms and everything around her disappeared. Well, until Callie barked and pulled at his pant leg.

"I see there's a dog in the bargain. She'll need to learn some manners."

"I can't wait to tell Joshua and Anna, and of course Katie. I need to wire my parents." Sophie laughed. “I wonder if Luke and Megan would be all right with a double wedding.”

“Not a chance. We’ll have the weddings a week apart.”

“Oh, Poor Clara.”

They walked hand in hand to the front porch of the ranch house. They couldn’t wait to surprise everyone with the news of their engagement. Before they went in, Wesley looked at Sophie with a tear in his eye. “Thank you for loving this broken man and healing my heart.

The End

Enjoy the first chapter of A Home For Her Heart

1891

Chapter One

Tears spilled down Ella's cheeks as Anna Wilson helped her step off the orphan train in Longview, Texas. She embraced the twelve-year-old girl. "What's wrong, Ella? Are you tired? I would understand if you were. We've traveled to so many towns in the last several weeks."

Ella wiped tears from her eyes. "No one wants me."

"I'm trying my best to find homes for each of you. You all deserve to have the love of a family." Anna hugged the six children in her care. "I have a good feeling about today. The last agent said several families' were waiting for the next orphan train."

Anna noticed Ella's flushed cheeks. "Ella, you look warm. Are you running a temperature?"

"I don't think so." Ella pulled at the front of her dress. "It's hot."

"This Texas humidity is suffocating." Anna laid her hand on Ella's forehead. "You're not running a temperature. I hope the people today understand what gifts each of you are. We're late, let's go find the opera house."

Anna followed the six children along the wooden sidewalk. Ella's red curls bounced with each step she took. Dust engulfed them from the passing horses and wagons. Michael coughed. *Did anyone ever get used to all this dirt?* Anna understood now why they covered the streets in New York with brick. It made walking so much easier. They passed by a bakery and the aroma of homemade bread made Anna's mouth water.

"I'm hungry. Can we buy sweet rolls, Miss Wilson?" Sam asked.

"I wish we had time. They smell wonderful." Anna spotted the opera house across the street. "We're almost there."

Anna opened the door of a two-story brick building and they walked in. Their train had arrived an hour late, and there were around twenty people waiting for them. There were more women than men sitting in groups and talking. A middle-aged man in a black suit came toward them.

"Welcome. I'm Pastor Williams and we've been expecting you." He held his hand out to Anna. "Did everyone have a pleasant trip?" He didn't wait for the children to respond. He asked Anna. "Are you comfortable introducing yourself?"

She shook his hand. "Yes to both questions and thank you. Children, please go sit in the chairs they've set out on stage."

Anna followed the children down the aisle, admiring the stained-glass windows of the Longview Opera House. There were four long windows on each side, and they cast shades of yellow, red, green and blue on the wooden floor in a kaleidoscope of colors. Each window depicted a scene from a famous play. It reminded Anna of the church her parents attended when she was a little girl. She hadn't been to church since then. Grief caught Anna by surprise and she had a difficult time holding back tears. Her parents had died eight years ago.

Her heart broke for each child on stage. Most of them had never known their parents, and the rest had lost theirs at a young age. The orphanage had provided the girls with white dresses, stockings, shoes and a bow for their hair. The four boys had on white shirts, jackets, knee pants, hats, socks and shoes. They looked adorable. Their sole possessions included one more outfit and a Bible.

Anna stepped to the front of the stage. She no longer got nervous speaking in front of people. Her concern for the children pushed her to overcome the anxiousness she used to feel.

"I want to thank everyone for coming. My name is Anna Wilson. I am an agent for the Children's Aid Society in New York City. We have traveled many miles to find families who will love these children. I care about each of them."

"They listen well and are considerate and loving. In the past, many people thought it appropriate to treat orphans as servants. I won't allow this." Anna glared at the audience. "I hope you'll love them as your own. Most of them were living on the streets before someone took them to the Children's Aid Society. They'd lost one or both parents and often their siblings. Their lives have been filled with difficulties and sorrow. My hope is you'll find it a privilege to provide a home for them. In return they'll show you how much it means to be a part of your family."

"When I finish speaking, I hope you'll talk with each child. I have a few rules," Anna studied the crowd. "I don't allow anyone to touch their muscles or look at their teeth. They're all healthy. Agents used to allow this, but I won't. They need respect. If you're interested in a child, I'll check with Longview's community leaders to find out if they believe your family would provide a good home. The children must feel comfortable around you, so I'll watch how you communicate and connect with them." She cleared her throat. "Could we get a drink of water? We had a long train ride and we're not used to this heat."

Pastor Williams left and returned with a bucket of water and a ladle.

"Thank you." Anna let the children drink first. She wished they had ice for the warm water, but it eased her parched throat.

"I'd like to introduce everyone. Children, please step forward when I say your name. First is Sam Foster, he's twelve." A lanky brown haired boy took his place by Anna. "A family in Opelousas, Louisiana took his younger brother Ben. They didn't have room for both boys. Sam has Ben's address so he can write to him. He wants to visit him one day. Their parents died in a factory fire when Sam was eight and Ben was five. Someone found them on the streets and brought them to the orphanage."

"Next is Ella Murphey, she's twelve." Ella stood next to Sam. She was taller than him and her red curls stuck out in every direction. Her cheeks grew pink which caused her freckles to appear darker. "Ella helps with the little ones. I don't know what I would've done without her. She doesn't remember her family. Her father brought her to the orphanage when she was three."

"Then we have Matthew, he's ten." He tried to go on the opposite side of Miss Wilson but Ella grabbed his arm and pulled him beside her. Matthew frowned at

Ella but recovered quickly and turned toward the audience and smiled, causing dimples to appear in his chubby cheeks. “His parents and siblings died from typhoid. A couple found him huddled in a corner of the apartment building they’d lived in and took him to the orphanage.”

Anna motioned to the small blonde-haired girl to stand next to her. “Laura is eight. When her parents didn’t return from a voyage to England, her grandmother cared for her. No one ever heard what happened to her parents. When her grandmother died Laura was only four. A family friend brought her to the orphanage.”

“Last are five-year-old twins, Scott and Michael.” They ran next to Laura. Each brother a mirror image of the other, black short hair, bright blue eyes and two missing top teeth. “If you’re thinking about taking them, I hope you’ll take both. Twins have a special connection. Their mother left them on the steps of the orphanage when they were babies. She’d pinned a note stating their names, and that she had no other choice. Thank you children, you can sit down. Does anyone have questions before you talk with them?” Anna watched a man get up and walk out. He wore torn jean overalls, and a ripped shirt. She wondered how often he bathed as there were dirt smudges across his face.

A woman with thick glasses stood up as she squinted at Anna. “If you’re not married can you care for a child?”

Anna scanned the crowd. She guessed most of them to be in their late twenties or early thirties, including the woman asking the question. “We prefer you’re married, but if you want to care for a child, we’re willing to let you try."

A man in a gray vest, jacket, matching trousers and black top hat stood, "Do you check on each child after they go with a family? What if a child is unhappy and doesn't want to stay in your home? Or if the families realize they can't care for them, how would you resolve it?"

"Yes, agents check on the children each time they bring new orphans. I'll be here for two weeks to make sure they're adjusting well and to make sure children from previous orphan trains are doing well. The agent after me should do the same. If a child is unhappy, we find another family for them. If we can't, we take them back to the Children's Aid Society in New York City. Children have run away from homes, and we've never heard from them again. We often learn afterward that those children were being physically or emotionally mistreated." Anna patted Scott's shoulder as he hopped from one foot to the other.

An older woman in the back row covered her mouth with her gloved hand. "Oh my, who would do such awful things?"

"Sometimes a neighbor or family member will do things in the privacy of their home you'd never imagine. I hope if you notice or hear something bad happening in a family, you'll report it. I'm glad most problems we have aren't so awful and are easily worked out." Anna paused and tucked a few loose strands of her toffee brown hair behind her ear. "Anyone else?" No one spoke. "If you come up with other questions, I'd love to answer them. Thank you for coming."

Anna paced the stage as people came to talk with

the children. It'd be difficult to let any of the children go. She'd come to love them. She walked over and stood in front of the curtain on the right side of the stage. She needed to get her emotions under control. Anna heard whispering behind her.

"Mary, what about the two girls?" A hoarse voice asked.

Anna noticed a hole in the curtain. She could see two older women through it.

"I'm not sure about the little girl, Bertha. The taller girl with red hair appears adequate." Mary glanced at the girls. "No one is saying anything to her, so you might be her only opportunity."

"I don't have time for nonsense. I need someone to do the housework I can no longer do. My health makes it difficult for me. I'm too old to take care of a child." Bertha sat in a wooden chair. It groaned and creaked beneath her. "She would have to follow my rules."

"Bertha, if she's in school, she can only help you in the evenings. And all children misbehave. I wonder if you have sufficient patience to have a child around, even an older one. Maybe this isn't the best solution for you." Mary sat next to her, clutching a big bag to her bosom.

"She doesn't need more school. She'll get real life experience taking care of a home. If she marries, she will need to know household management." Bertha scooted back in her chair, a snap caused her to stand abruptly, as the chair broke into pieces all over the floor. "They sure don't make chairs like they used to."

Anna had heard enough. She went around the curtain. "I overheard your conversation, and I won't let Ella leave with you. As I expressed in my introduction, they're not servants. They need love and a family. Ella is a lovely and helpful girl. She deserves more than someone who wants a housekeeper. You should both leave."

"Of all the nerve. Mary, let's go." Bertha's face turned red. "The mayor will hear about this. I wanted to help that child, and this is how I'm treated." Bertha waddled down the stairs, huffing and puffing her way through the people and out the door. Mary followed behind her.

Anna's heart raced as she walked back to the front of the stage. Her nails dug into her palms as she clenched her hands into fists. Her cheeks were on fire and she knew her face was red. *I can't believe how selfish people are. Ella deserves a real family.*

The well-dressed man who had asked the questions earlier approached Anna. He was holding hands with an attractive women. "Miss Wilson, my name is Thomas Gage, and this is my wife, Emma." He shook Anna's hand. "We're interested in providing a home for the twins. In our five years of marriage we haven't been blessed with children. Our home is nice and we have four bedrooms. I'm the town doctor and my wife would stay with them."

Anna drew a deep breath. "I appreciate you wanting to provide a home for them but are you aware of how rambunctious two little boys can be? They might destroy something valuable. If you had children of your own, would you still want the twins? Or would they be a burden to you?" Anna glared at Emma.

"Oh no, Miss Wilson, we'd think of the boys as ours." Mrs. Gage paused. "They'd be the older siblings to any child we might have. Once you give a child your heart, you wouldn't take it back. I assure you, God gives us enough love for everyone in our lives." She clutched her husband's hand as if clinging to a lifeline.

"I wonder if God bothers with such matters. He allowed their parents to give them away." Anna took a few deep breaths, to calm herself down. "I'm sorry if I sound cynical. Before I came over here, I overheard a conversation which upset me. My recommendation would be to take Michael and Scott for two hours today. When you're done, bring them to our hotel and you can do the same for the next few days. You could increase the time you have them each day. As long as everything goes well for the twins and both of you, we'll talk about a permanent arrangement." Anna smiled.

Mrs. Gage's expression softened. "Oh, what a wonderful idea. It'd give us time to get our home prepared." She glanced up at her husband. "What do you think, Thomas?"

"It's a good plan. We'll get to know them and they can decide if they want to live with us. Would it be all right if we took them to lunch and to our house to play? We have a large yard and a new furry puppy." Mr. Gage lifted his hat and wiped his forehead with a handkerchief.

"Let me talk with the boys. I'll be right back." Anna walked over to Michael and Scott. "There's a couple who wishes to have lunch with you both. After eating they'll take you to their home to play with their new puppy for a while. Would you like to go with them?"

"Yes, Miss Wilson," Michael gave her a toothless smile.

Scott nodded. "I would love to play with a puppy."

"When you are through playing, they'll bring you to the hotel. You'll have lots of fun." Anna walked back with the boys to give the good news to Mr. and Mrs. Gage.

***

"Well girls, let's eat supper and find our hotel. Our luggage should be there." Anna took each girl by the hand. "I can't say I'm sorry the right family didn't come for you both. Now I have more time with you. We'll stay here for two weeks. Our next and last stop will be in Nacogdoches, Texas. I believe families are waiting there for both of you."

"It's all right Miss Wilson. No one wants me. They don't even speak to me. I'll go back to the orphanage with you." Ella wiped tears away.

"No one wants me either. They only take boys. I'm happy Sam, Matthew and the twins found families but why don't they like girls, Miss Wilson?" Laura looked up at Anna with her big blue eyes brimming with unshed tears. "Doesn't God want us to find a family?"

Anna's heart broke. The girls' lives had been full of disappointments. Every time she paraded them in front of families, their hopes were high they'd find a home. When they didn't, rejection and disappointment settled on them.

Anna understood their responses. She'd experienced pain when the man she'd loved rejected her for someone else. At twenty-nine her prospects of finding love were slim. She resented the label of spinster, but it applied to her. Anna wanted a family but how could she ever trust a man with her heart again?

She needed a plan to take care of these precious girls. Ella's chances of someone wanting her for more than a housekeeper or nanny weren't good, as Anna had witnessed today. Laura wasn't as old, but girls weren't valued as highly as boys. The West needed laborers. Boys grew up and helped on the homesteads.

"Oh girls, you're beautiful. If the right family comes along, they'll love you as much as I do. I'm certain God wants you both to find families. Why wouldn't He? You're angels. After supper let's eat ice cream. It's been a long day and you both deserve a treat." Anna bent and wiped the tears away and kissed them on the cheek. "No more crying. It's time for fun."

Ella hugged Anna tight. "I wish we could stay with you, Miss Wilson."

"Me too." Laura joined in the hug.

"Me too." Anna whispered to herself.

~

The rocking rhythm of the train lolled Ella and Laura to sleep for most of the journey from Longview to Nacogdoches, Texas. Anna enjoyed looking out the window as forests and lakes sped by. She caught a whiff of coffee brewing in the dining car. Her stomach rumbled.

"Next stop Nacogdoches. Please prepare to disembark." The conductor announced.

Being an agent gave Anna the ability to travel and see places, but it didn't pay enough for her to live on her own. Maybe she should check into getting a teaching certificate and moving out West with the girls to teach.

Screeches and squeals from the train brakes startled Anna from her thoughts, and she looked outside at the depot coming into view.

Ella sat up, rubbing her eyes. "Are we there?"

"I believe so. We'll pick up our baggage and go to the hotel. I didn't know when we'd arrive when I sent out the telegram, so we won't be meeting with families until tomorrow." Anna stood. The girls followed her down the aisle.

"What a beautiful town." Anna glanced around at the small crowd as she stepped off the train. The smell of pine filled the air and evergreen trees stood as strong sentinels overlooking the area.

"It's pretty, Miss Wilson, so many trees. It's hot here too, but I like it. There's lots of shade." Ella stepped off the train.

Anna helped Laura down the steps. "Do you like it?"

"I do." Laura grabbed Ella's hand and smiled. "We'll meet our families here, Ella."

Ella stared at the ground. "You will, Laura."

"We need to get our luggage and find the hotel." Anna stepped backward and tripped over a satchel on the ground behind her. She tried regaining her balance, but instead strong arms wrapped around her waist. However, they didn't stop her fall. She landed on top of a muscular man.

"Oh my," Anna tried to push herself up. *Where should she place her hands so she wouldn't touch the man underneath her?* Her cheeks were on fire and people were starring.

"Miss Wilson, are you okay? That sure was funny," Ella giggled. "Grab my hands and I'll pull you up."

Anna made it to her feet and straightened her skirt. She turned around to thank the man who broke her fall. He wore jeans, brown cowboy boots and a white shirt. Dark brown hair waved from under his white cowboy hat. When she found the courage to look into his face, a pair of ice-blue eyes looked amused at her embarrassment. "I'm so sorry. I didn't check behind me before I backed up," she stammered. "Did I hurt you?"

"I'm fine, miss. Someone as slim as you wouldn't hurt me. I tried catching you but it didn't go as intended. Are you all right?" He held out his hand. "My name is Joshua."

Anna shook his hand. "I'm Anna Wilson and nothing is hurt, thanks to you. Glad you didn't hurt your head or break anything."

Joshua picked up the satchel. "It's dented. Is it yours?"

"It isn't. I wonder who'd sit a bag down and walk off?" Anna scanned the crowd, but no one rushed to claim the satchel. "I guess we should leave it, in case they come back. Do you know if they're unloading the luggage yet?"

Joshua sat the satchel on the ground. "We can find out. I need to get my mother's trunks. Follow me and I'll load your bags into your wagon."

"Oh, I wouldn't want to bother you with our bags. I'm sure you're busy, and we don't have a wagon. I'll hire someone to take our bags to the Grand Hotel." Anna took the girl's hands. "We'll follow you, though."

"It's no problem. I'll load your bags into my wagon and drop them off at the hotel. Which ones are yours? I'd offer you all a ride, but I'm out of room. My mother is coming to live with me and she brought enough trunks to fill two wagons. Which won't leave space for young ladies, sorry to say."

Anna tried to keep up with him. "Please don't bother about us. The girls and I like to walk. We'll get to see part of the town."

Joshua walked toward the men unloading luggage from the train to the wooden platform. He found his mother's trunks while Anna and the girls searched for theirs.

"We sat our luggage over there." Anna pointed to the bags. "Thank you again for helping us."

"You're welcome." Joshua smiled.

Anna's breath caught. Joshua had dimples, and his smile made her pulse pick up a beat or two. "Where is the Grand Hotel?"

"Turn right at the end of this street. It's three blocks down Main Street to the left. Have a good day ladies. It's nice to meet you." Joshua grabbed the bags.

"It was nice meeting you as well. Let's find the hotel, girls." Anna walked away but couldn't help taking one last glance at her rescuer. He was watching them. Their eyes met. Anna turned back around. *I'm sure he's married and has a family.*

She needed to accept her life. Her days would be filled with finding a home for the girls and checking on the children from previous orphan trains. Who had time for men, even the kind and handsome cowboy type men? He'd only end up breaking her heart.

Read the rest here

Darlia Sawyer grew up living in many of the western states during her childhood. She now lives in Western Colorado and considers it to be a blessing. Beautiful scenery, rich history and great weather to enjoy it all in.

She lost her husband of twenty years in 2004 after dealing with medical issues his whole life. Her relationship with Jesus and her daughter and two sons helped her through those days.

She married Ken in 2007 and together they have three boys and three girls, just like the Brady Bunch. All the children are now adults and they've added two son-in-law's and two adorable granddaughters to the family. Next year we'll be adding two more grandbabies and a daughter-in-law.

There have always been two constants in her life. The love and strength found in her relationship with her Heavenly Father and her love for writing and history.

The support from her husband, Ken, has given her the opportunity to follow her lifelong dream of writing full time.

She hopes her writing will inspire hope, a passion for life and the chance to once again believe in miracles.

To find this book and others by Darlia Sawyer, visit her at:
https://amazon.com/author/darliasawyer
Also you can follow her on Amazon and other social media"
https://www.facebook.com/DarliaSawyerAuthor
https://twitter.com/DarliaSawyer
https://www.instagram.com/darliasawyer